EDITED BY Bill Pronzini
AND Martin H. Greenberg

INTRODUCTION BY Robert E. Briney

# THE BEST WESTERN STORIES OF
# LEWIS B. PATTEN

D0101095

G.K.HALL &CO.
Boston, Massachusetts
1989

Published in Large Print by arrangement with
Ohio University Press.

G.K. Hall Large Print Book Series.

Set in 16 pt Plantin.

---

*Library of Congress Cataloging in Publication Data*

Patten, Lewis B.
  The best western stories of Lewis B. Patten / edited by Bill
Pronzini and Martin H. Greenberg : introduction by Robert E.
Briney.
        p.       cm.—(Nightingale series) (G.K. Hall large print book
series)
  ISBN 0-8161-4781-7 (lg. print)
  1. Western stories.   2. Large type books.      I. Pronzini, Bill.
II. Greenberg, Martin Harry.      III. Title.
[PS3566.A79A6    1989]
813'.54—dc19                                                88-34935

---

# Contents

# Introduction
## THE TALL QUIET MAN
### By Robert E. Briney

Lewis Patten's first published story, "Too Good with a Gun," appeared in the April 1950 issue of *Zane Grey's Western Magazine*. When the magazine's editor announced the story in the preceding issue as by "a promising new writer," he could not have known how prodigally that promise would be fulfilled. Several more Patten stories appeared in that same year, and for the next half dozen years Patten was a frequent and popular contributor to most of the Western pulp magazines, as well as to "quality" magazines such as the *Colorado Quarterly*.

His first novel was published in 1952. By the time the Western pulps (and indeed most other fiction magazines) had disappeared from the nation's newsstands a few years later, Patten was well established as a writer of Western novels for both hardback and paperback publishers. Throughout a thirty-one-year career during which he produced

1

over a hundred novels, he maintained consistently high ratings from both reviewers and readers. His short fiction has been reprinted in anthologies and his work has been adapted for television and theatrical films. His novels have been reprinted in numerous editions in paperback and have been translated into eleven languages. Patten was a three-time winner of the best-of-the-year Spur Award from the Western Writers of America, and in 1979, close to the end of his career, he received that organization's Golden Saddleman Award for his contributions to Western fiction.

Lewis Byford Patten was born in Denver, Colorado, on January 13, 1915. He grew up in that city and attended Denver University. At the age of eighteen he enlisted in the United States Navy. He served in the Asiatic Fleet, mostly in China and the Philippines, from 1933 to 1937. In December 1938 he married Betsy Lancaster. (The marriage lasted for twenty-four years, ending in divorce in 1962. The Pattens had one daughter, Frances Ann, and two sons, Clifford and Lewis B., Jr. In July 1963 Patten married Catherine Crane, a teacher.) In 1941 Patten went to work for the Colorado Department of Revenue and over the next two years rose to the position of senior auditor.

Having had his fill of bureaucracy, in 1943 Patten moved his family to a farm in DeBeque, in western Colorado, where he spent the next six years as a farmer and rancher. In May 1949, "having decided that ranching involved too damn much work for the return," Patten left the ranch and made a bid for a career as a full-time writer. His break came on September 26, 1949, with the arrival of a $75.00 check for "Too Good with a Gun," together with a friendly and encouraging letter from Don Ward, the editor of *Zane Grey's Western Magazine*. That first sale, which appears as the first story in the present collection, was later selected by Western writer Luke Short for his anthology *Bad Men and Good* (1953) and was adapted as an episode of "The General Electric Theater," the long-running series on CBS television.

It would still be some time before writing paid off steadily enough to support Patten and his family. There would be lean periods when he would have to take other jobs to keep solvent. But he kept a photograph of that first check on his office wall as proof that he had finally found his true career. As for the check itself, Patten recalled its fate in a note written for the WWA journal *The Roundup* (March 1971): "I happened to be away from the house that day [at the Denver Union Stockyards with a cattleman and former neighbor]. My wife got the mail and opened the envelope. Before I came home, she had called about a dozen friends and organized a party for that night to celebrate. Easy come, easy go. The check paid for the party."

The first sale was quickly followed by others, and at least seven Patten stories had appeared in print by the end of 1950. In addition to *Zane Grey's Western Magazine*, the list of magazines carrying Patten fiction, from short stories to book-length tales, is virtually a catalogue of the newsstand Western magazines of the 1950s: *Best Western, Complete Western Book Magazine, Exciting Western, Fifteen Western Tales, .44 Western Magazine, Giant Western, Mammoth Western, Popular Western, Texas Rangers, Thrilling Ranch Stories, Thrilling Western, Western Short Stories, Western Story*, and undoubtedly others.

In 1952 Ace Books published Patten's first novel, *Massacre at White River*, as the fourth in the series of Ace Double Novels (two novels, usually by different authors, bound back-to-back in a single paperback volume). His second book, *Gunmen's Grass*, was also a paperback (Popular Library, 1954), published under the penname Lewis Ford. (The story had previously appeared in the April 1953 *Giant Western* under the title "Blood on the Grass," also as by Lewis Ford.) Two further Lewis Ford paperbacks were published. Later in the 1950s, Patten collaborated with his friend and fellow Western writer, Wayne D. Overholser, on three novels that were published under Overholser's pennames Joseph Wayne and Lee Leighton. Patten also wrote two Gene Autry juveniles and a Jim Bowie adventure for Whitman Publishing Company. By 1960 the flirting with pseudonyms was over, and the remainder of Patten's work appeared under his own name.

Patten was a steady and reliable writer. Once he hit his stride, a typical year would see the publication of from three to five new Patten books. (In 1957 the total reached eight.) He wrote for at least eighteen publishers in the United States and eight in England. In 1963 he began a long association with Doubleday & Co., which published thirty-two of his novels over the next eighteen years. Patten's other major publisher was New American Library (Signet Books), which published more than two dozen titles, both paperback orginals and reprints of the Doubleday hardbacks. These paperbacks went through numerous editions, and a rotating selection of titles was kept in print throughout the 1960s and 1970s.

In addition to his writing, Patten also found time for activities such as hunting, fishing, camping, travel, and a reputed average of eighteen holes of golf each morning before starting the day's writing. He liked Mexico, and he and his wife travelled there often to fish and relax between books. He was a charter member of the Western Writers of America and was active in that organization throughout his career—he helped to organize the first WWA convention, served on the governing board and on numerous committees, contributed to *The Roundup* (everything from reminiscences to polemics), and ran unsuccessfully for president in 1971. He was also active in a Denver-area writer's group called the Bull Wranglers.

Patten was known as "Pat" to his friends, who described him as a quiet man, slow to anger but a fighter when aroused, intensely serious, and somewhat of a loner. According to Ray Gaulden (*The Roundup*, July/August 1981) he was "always willing to lend a hand; never reluctant to have a say on issues that didn't meet with his approval."

In the February 1979 *Roundup*, Patten described his working methods. "My work habits are rigid. I sit in an easy chair and type on a very low table in front of me, a table that has compartments for paper, envelopes, etc. My day's quota is half a chapter, or about four and half closely typed pages. When my quota is done, I quit. And until the last two or three years, I never missed a day of work.

"Each morning before beginning to write, I read the previous day's work and edit it. In fact, I usually edit each page at least five times before I send the book out to be typed. But I rarely re-write, and when I do, it is only the first two or three pages of a book.

"I have always maintained that there are thousands of potential writers with more talent than I have. What they don't have is guts: the will to sit down at the typewriter and write, whether the copy that comes out is worth a damn or not. If they keep trying, sooner or later it *will* be worth a damn and some publisher will buy it."

Patten's success in the marketplace was matched by awards from his peers. In 1969 he received WWA's Spur Award for *The Red Sabbath* as the best Western historical novel of the preceding year. This is a "Custer novel," treating the events surrounding the battle of the Little Big Horn from the point of view of a hard-bitten civilian scout. Also in 1969, Patten's *Bones of the Buffalo* (1967) appeared on a WWA list of "ten Westerns no library should be without."

In his first novel, Patten had dealt with the Ute Indian uprising along the Colorado/Utah border in 1879, in which Indian agent Nathan Meeker and most of the personnel of the White River Agency were killed. Patten's friend Wayne Overholser had also used this historical event in several of his novels. In 1969 the two writers collaborated on *The Meeker Massacre*, a retelling of this story for young readers. This collaboration received the Spur Award in 1970 for best Western juvenile novel.

Patten received his third Spur Award in 1973 for *A Killing in Kiowa* (1972), which tells of the aftermath of a killing by four drunken teen-agers in a frontier town. The deck is stacked against the sheriff in his attempt to bring the boys to justice, because the fathers of three of them are the most powerful rancher in the area, the local banker, and the sheriff's own deputy.

A number of Patten's short stories were adapted for television, and three of his books were turned into movies. The best, and best-known, of the latter is *Death of a Gunfighter* (1968), the story of a trail-town marshal who discovers that he has outlived his time and that his gun skills are no longer wanted by the town. The movie, released by Universal-International in 1969, featured Richard Widmark and Lena Horne. Other Patten books that were filmed are *Gun Proud* (1957), which became *Red Sundown* (1956), with Rory Calhoun and Martha Hyer, and *The Killer from Yuma* (1964), which became an Italian/West German/Spanish co-production called *Don't Turn the Other Cheek (1971)*, with Franco Nero and Eli Wallach.

At its annual convention in June 1979, the Western Writers of America presented the organization's Golden Saddleman Award to Lewis B. Patten. (He had also been nominated for the award in 1978, when it went to A. B. Guthrie, Jr.) The award is sponsored jointly with the Levi Straus Company, and is intended to recognize the recipient's "contribution to Western history and legend." The nomination statement in the May 1979 issue of *The Roundup* said in part: "Lewis eptomizes the tall quiet man of so many of his fictional protagonists. Inwardly he is intensively serious, and a gifted novelist with a tremendous drive. . . . It is well that within WWA is a hard core of the type of professionals who started Western Writers of America, and have given the organization its salt, and its character. Lewis Patten stands tall and strong in the unique fraternity he has had such a tremendous hand in fashioning and building."

By the time his last novel, *Ride a Tall Horse*, was published in July 1980, Patten had been diagnosed as a victim of lung cancer. Ironically, although Patten had given up smoking many years earlier—he quit cold-turkey one Saturday night on the way home from a meeting of the Bull Wranglers—the doctors blamed the cancer on this long-past tobacco habit. Lengthy treatment, including frequent hospitalization and radical lung surgery, failed to halt the progress of the disease. After his surgery, Patten was able to make a last visit to Mexico. He came back with plans for another visit, but it was not to be. The author of more than a hundred successful and highly rated Western novels died on May 22, 1981, at the age of sixty-six.

Lewis B. Patten was a teller of well-constructed tales, framed by a tough-minded sensibility and set forth in crisp, efficient prose. Although he chose to work within the framework of the traditional or popular Western adventure novel, he had a talent for casting new light on standard ingredients and peopling his stories with fresh and interesting characters. His protagonists are often prey to uncertainties and ignoble impulses. Many of his villains are ordinary men acting out of honest conviction or understandable weakness rather than evil nature. His books often deal with themes such as prejudice, mob psychology and its consequences, and the degenerating effects of guilt and fear. There is little or no humor. Patten's West is a gritty and violent place, where bad things happen to good people, where innocent or justified acts can have disproportionately harsh consequences, where victory exacts a price.

In many of his best works, the protagonist is an adolescent, forced into situations he is ill-prepared to handle. In *Rope Law*

(1956), eleven-year old Joe Redenko catches the local banker making a clandestine visit to Joe's mother and warns him away, making a lifelong enemy. The banker's persecution almost drives the embittered boy into outlawry, from which an elderly sheriff tries to save him. In *Top Man with a Gun* (1959) the sixteen-year-old protagonist seeks revenge for the killing of his father and sister, while in *The Ordeal of Jason Ord* (1973), the teen-age hero struggles against a false accusation of murder. In *The Gun of Jesse Hand* (1973), townsmen turn against seventeen-year-old Jesse when he kills two men in self-defense after they have murdered an old Indian. Jesse's skill with a gun causes the "good" citizens to reject him, and, goaded by manipulative "friends" and employers, he follows an ever more violent path.

Another frequent Patten character is the honest lawman forced into conflict with the people who hired him by his refusal to bow to local prejudices or vested interests. Samples of this theme are found in *Rope Law* (1956), *The Law in Cottonwood* (1978), and *A Killing in Kiowa* (1972). Not all lawmen are honest, of course, but the venal and crooked ones (*The Ruthless Range* [1963], *The Gun of Jesse Hand* [1973]) are in the minority. In *The Tarnished Star* (1963), the sheriff of a small town becomes a drunkard and lawless elements take over, until the sheriff's son decides to restore the integrity of the badge.

Patten also dealt in many books with Indian battles, both historical—the Ute wars, the battle of the Little Big Horn, the Fetterman massacre (*Massacre Ridge* [1971]), the seige of Beecher's Island (*Red Runs the River* [1970])—and fictional, as in *Apache Hostage* (1969) and *Ambush at Soda Creek* (1976). In the latter book, a vengeful Indian scout leads three cavalry troops in pursuit of a band of Apaches who are using the commanding officer's kidnapped wife as bait to draw the cavalry into an ambush. In a number of books, such as *The Killings at Coyote Springs* (1977), it is the white settlers who commit violence against the Indians. In *A Death in Indian Wells* (1970), buffalo hunters kill a young Cheyenne, putting the local tribe into conflict with the small Kansas town of Indian Wells. In the middle of the conflict is the sheriff, who is married to a Cheyenne woman and whose deputy is his nineteen-year-old half-Cheyenne son. Of all the characters in these books, the ones who are portrayed most unsympathetically are the professional Indian fighters, especially glory-hunting cavalry officers.

A sampling of other Patten books will show the variety of his work: the attempt to smuggle gold from the West back to the Confederacy during the Civil War (*Wagons East* [1964]); a feud between two families that leads to a tragic suicide pact and its violent aftermath (*Showdown at Mesilla* [1971]); an unusual posse, including a beautiful woman, which complicates the sheriff's task in hunting down a trio of bank robbers (*Posse from Poison Creek* [1969]); a gunman attempting to outrun his past (*The Ruthless Range* [1963]); a band of United States outlaws in Mexico attempting to steal money from Pancho Villa (*Villa's Rifles* [1971]); the bitter hatred of a reluctant frontier wife for her husband, which turns one of their sons into a murderer who is ready to destroy his own family (*Six Ways of Dying* [1970]); townsmen who have convicted and hanged an innocent man and are now reminded of their shameful act by the return of the victim's son (*Guilt of a Killer Town* [1971]).

The women in Patten's work range from the pure sweetheart, whose faith strengthens the hero, to the town hussy, from the demure young woman waiting patiently on the sidelines to the active helpmate and partner. In several books women are victims of violence: kidnapping by outlaws, capture by Indians, rape, and even murder. It is her rape by a drunken gang that crystalizes the wife's hatred for her husband in *Six Ways of Dying*. In *Ruthless Range* the young wife of the gunman protagonist runs away from him in search of the security and stability he cannot provide, only to turn up later as a prostitute after being sexually victimized by a man she trusted. When such violence occurs, however, it is in the service of strong drama (and occasionally melodrama) and Patten's grim view of the West, rather than mere sensationalism.

It cannot be claimed that all of Patten's books meet his generally high level of quality. As is not unexpected for so prolific a writer, a number of his books show signs of haste: subsidiary characters (and sometimes even major participants) only sketchily drawn, plot developments unresolved (for example, the dishonest sheriff in *The Ruthless Range*, last seen trying to kill the hero, simply disappears from the book and is not mentioned again), the hero's multiple problems cleared up with unrealistic ease in the final pages. But Patten was never less than a competent craftsman, and even in books that are not among his best one can enjoy the brisk pace, vivid action, moments of honest but well-controlled emotion, and the occasional flash of the unpredictable in people or plot.

Most of the themes and qualities of Patten's novels can be found in his short fiction as well, sometimes with an added intimacy provided by the smaller canvas. In his first story he dealt with a common character in the traditional Western: the man who is skilled with a gun, self-doubting ("I reckon a man gets along better in this world if he don't use a gun too good.") but still hoping to find people who will look at the uses to which the skill is put rather than just at the skill itself. One of those uses is revenge, and this is the central theme in Patten's second story, "Massacre at Cottonwood Springs." Like these first few stories, five of the other entries in this collection center around deadly encounters and the ways in which the violence changes the participants. In the three remaining stories violence is avoided, or at least kept off-stage.

In "Dobbs Ferry" the wife learns the virtues of "bread cast upon the waters," while the husband *may* have learned to be less foolishly trusting. In "High-Carded" (published in magazine form as "Fast Draw Feud") a sheriff's deputy sent to bring in his own brother recalls crucial events from their shared past and learns a belated lesson. In "The Rough String" (also published under the title "Big Black and the Bully") a young boy and his father help each other to learn courage in the face of fear. Twelve-year-old Ernie, in "Nester Kid," displays a fully formed courage, and it is others who learn from it. The fearlessness of old Pete Handy in "The Winter of His Life" may have kindled a spark in a young man's mind. And in "Payday" a glimpse of another man's happiness drives the bitterness out of a man, rather than increasing it. In each case, violence or the threat of violence teaches a lesson.

The two longest stories in this collection are closer in spirit to Patten's novels. "They Called Him a Killer" is a taut tale of suspense in which the Western trappings are not essential. Lloyd Cannon was convicted and imprisoned for the murder of his wife, but claimed not to remember the act. Many years later he escapes, apparently for the purpose of tracking down the real murderer.

The man sent after him, to return him to prison before he gets himself killed, is Cannon's son, who believes his father guilty. Finally, in "Hell-Bent" a bankrupt rancher learns how viciously his former neightbors will turn on him now that he is no longer a power in the community.

Let these stories introduce you to Lewis B. Patten, the tall quiet man, and one of the most popular practitioners of the traditional Western story.

# Too Good with a Gun

They rode through the thin warmth of this bright winter's day, a man and a girl, together on the bouncing seat of the greyed and weathered buckboard, very concious of one another each time their bodies touched, laughing and red of face by turns.

Behind rode the boy, Claude, jogging gently in the rising dust. Suddenly he tugged at his sorrel's reins and as the horse fell behind, called to Russ Baker, "I'll catch up later," his fifteen-year-old mind dimly shocked by the man's antics.

Shaking out his rope, he dropped an experimental loop over a nearby clump of greasewood, rearing back in the saddle to tighten it as the blocky mustang braced to a stop.

He slid off the horse, running as he hit the ground. Grinning triumphantly, he reached the end of the tightened lariat in a matter of seconds. Pulling slack into the rope, he loosened the loop and slipped it off the spiny brush, then tensed abruptly and fell into a half-crouch. Easily, still crouching, he turned and his slim brown hand dropped swiftly. His gun cleared its holster and racketed across the wide valley as it bucked in his hand. A rock across the road shot off dust and Claude grinned widely now as he holstered his gun.

The horse, startled, was moving away trailing the lariat in the dust. Claude broke into a run, caught the end of the rope and, jerking on it, yelled, "Whoa. Steady now."

The horse turned to face him obediently, backing gently as slack came into the rope. Again the boy let the grin cross his narrow, smooth face and he tipped his hat back on his head and swaggered to the horse, coiling the rope as he went. He mounted, kicked the horse into a run, and with a yell took after the buckboard.

He had meant to ride up behind the buckboard, shooting and yelling as a badman might, attacking a stage, but the sight of Russ Baker, blushing and grinning foolishly beside Claude's sister Edie, changed his mind and brought a look of disgust to his face. He felt ashamed for Russ and the shame touched him too, so great was his liking and respect for the man. That this slim, taciturn rider should let a slip of a girl change him was beyond belief.

He came up behind, not noticing the dust, and let his horse trot, its muzzle a foot from the rear of the buckboard. His head dropped onto his chest in an attitude of bored relaxation, but the eyes were alive and bright in their blackness and occasionally the full lips moved, tightening or twisting. Once he snarled under his breath, "Draw, you dirty sidewinder," his hand hanging clawlike over the holstered grip of his gun and his body growing tense.

The town of Four-Mile came into sight and Russ slowed the team. Edie brushed the dust carefully from her clothes and took on a prim expression and sat in the far corner of the seat, away from Russ.

Claude never paid much attention to Edie, but as she got down in front of Hatfield's store and walked across the board sidewalk, he noticed how pretty she was. Maybe it was the soft expression on her face or the way she moved her body, feeling Russ Baker's eyes upon her.

Claude was dismounting, eyeing the green batwing doors of the saloon, and he wondered how long it would be before he could drum up enough nerve to walk down there

21

and go through them. Russ tied the team to the rail and Claude climbed up in the seat beside him. Russ looked at the boy, grinning with the hard, tight muscles of his face.

"Jist as well take it easy, Claude. She'll be a while."

Claude looked at this man, seeing him now as he had always been, without the change on him that came when he was with Edie. He said, "I busted a rock back there, drawin' an' whirlin' at the same time," unconscious of the pride in his voice, his eyes waiting for the man's approbation. Instead he saw the uneasiness and the regret coming into Russ's face and the man spoke softly.

"Your pa an' ma feel pretty strong about gunfightin'. They give you that gun for varmints, not men. They jumped all over me for teachin' you as much as I have. You'd best forget it. I reckon a man gets along better in this world if he don't use a gun too good."

He stopped and the feeling that he was talking too much was plain on him but he still had something on his mind, something that rankled within him. "Your pa thinks, an' mebbe he's right, that I'm too good with my gun to be good for Edie."

Claude thought about that, thought about how right Pa was most of the time, thought about how much he liked this lanky puncher. He wished Pa could see Russ like he did. He saw the brightness of Edie's dress through the open door of the store, saw the heavy shape of Mr. Hatfield beside her. He took his eyes away, letting them drift on down the street again toward the saloon and he felt the helplessness in him because of his age.

He said with a surly impatience, "A man ought to know how to use a gun."

A horseman came down the street and dismounted behind the buckboard, tying his horse beside Claude's at the hitchrail. He grinned at Claude and came over, a friendly man, well liked and universally respected. He wore a gun, as most men did, but it was rusty.

Arnold Hoffman put a big calloused hand on Claude's shoulder and said, "How are you, boy? How's your pa an' ma?" but then Russ turned and the man forgot Claude and said, "I'll buy you a drink, Russ."

Russ started to move and then, looking at the doorway of the store, shook his head, "Another time. I'm waiting for Edie."

Claude felt his throat tightening and he

wanted to say, "I'll drink with you," but he couldn't make his voice come out. In a moment it was too late and Arnold was striding away. Now the boy made his lips move: *I'll drink with you*, silently, and after clearing his throat, again: "I'll drink with you," his face consciously without expression.

Russ turned. "What did you say?" But Claude only got hot and red of face. He muttered, "Nothin'."

Old man Hatfield's voice droned on inside the store and after a while another man came from the hotel and stopped on his way to the saloon to stand in front of the buckboard and stare hard at Russ.

His voice had a soft, sibilant sound to it. "Russ Baker! I'll be damned. You're a long ways from home."

Claude felt the tightening and the straightening up of the man in the seat beside him. He heard a voice but it did not sound like Russ's usual, easy drawl.

Russ said, "Hello, Slick," and the silence grew heavy as the two men stared, warily and with obvious dislike of one another. Then the other man, thin and sardonic of face, went on by and entered the saloon. There was something about him that lin-

24

gered behind, making Claude feel uneasy without knowing why.

He asked, strongly curious, "You know him, Russ? He's a stranger here."

"Knew him in Texas. Slick Everitt."

Claude whistled. "The gunfighter?" and when Russ nodded, a boy's awe came into Claude's face. He had not seen anything prepossessing about Everitt but the man had a reputation that was well known. He said, "Gee, I hope I get to be as good as him someday."

Russ laughed, a harsh, bitter laugh. "No. Not 'as good as him,' boy, because there ain't no 'good' in him. He's a human rattlesnake and there ain't a bit more feelin' in him than in a snake."

The minutes ran on, dragged into an hour, but Everitt had left something behind with the two on the buckboard seat. They could not take their minds from him. Edie came out once, smiling at them, and put some packages into the buckboard.

When she saw their faces she said, "Don't look so grim. It won't be long now."

After a while over the stillness of the street, Claude heard a table crash to the floor in the saloon and afterward an angry shout. Then he heard the low murmur of a man's voice, steadily cursing. An uneasiness touched him and he felt Russ straightening up beside him.

The batwings of the saloon swung open and Arnold Hoffman and the gunfighter, Everitt, came out together, propelled by Big Nick Bidwell, the saloonman, who had a huge, powerful hand grasping each of their arms. The steady cursing came from Everitt, bubbling from his thin lips in a revolting stream. Hoffman wore an angry flush on his ordinarily open and friendly face.

Big Nick growled, "I had that back-bar mirror freighted from Salt Lake. I'll not have it broken now."

Everitt left off his cursing long enough to say, "I'll settle you when I'm through with this one."

Big Nick gave a little shove and the man staggered across the walk, nearly falling as he went into the street. He swung, crouching, the bright eyes resting on Big Nick for a moment and then going to Hoffman.

Russ Baker was moving next to Claude. He was down off the buckboard and around in front of the horses before Claude was scarcely aware of his movement. Everitt had his pale eyes on Arnold Hoffman and he stood there in an easy way, but tense and sure.

He said, "You want to tangle with me and you got a gun. Use it." As he watched Arnold his eyes betrayed a hot and vicious pleasure.

Claude could see surprise and sudden knowledge of how this argument must end in Arnold's face. Arnold knew he was up against a gunfighter and he knew that he would die. Claude watched the play of expression on the man's face, felt a little sickened as he saw it go gray with fear, felt the man's shame with him for a moment, and then saw the hopeless courage come into his eyes. He moved his glance to Everitt and saw the evil there in the predatory, waiting stance, in the pale eyes. He thought of a rattler and saw no more pity here than he would in a striking snake.

He felt a little sick, knowing that Arnold would die, but then Russ called out, "Slick. Turn around this way."

Slick Everitt spoke without turning. "This ain't none of your business, Baker. Keep out of it."

Russ's voice had a slow, deep quality. "No. This ain't my business. Somethin' else is. I told you once that there isn't a town

27

big enough for the both of us. Reckon you forgot. You won't again."

Some of the sureness went out of Everitt as he faced Russ. The surprise that came to his face as Russ spoke puzzled Claude as did his words, never finished, "You're a liar. You never—"

Russ cut him short: "All right. All right. You've said enough."

Arnold's relief and gratitude were naked things, unconcealed as his face trembled in the extremity of his emotion. Russ kept his eyes steadily on Slick. Claude had felt proud and less afraid as Russ called to the killer but now his fear came back tenfold, fear for his friend.

He saw a bright movement behind Russ in the door of the store and Edie came out onto the walk. Russ said irritably, "Edie, get back in the store," but Edie just stood there, uncomprehending, until Hoffman caught her arm and pulled her in.

Claude's thoughts cried out. *Why'd you do it, Russ? Why'd you step into Arnold's fight? Now it's you that's—*

Things happened fast then. Claude's last impression was of the pitiless evil in the gun fighter's eyes and of surprise that Russ did not show more change. Then the guns came

28

out and spoke across the narrow distance between the two, Russ's a shade faster, Everitt's so close afterward that the two reports nearly mingled. But the shock of Russ's bullet spoiled the other's aim. The evil and the life went out of Everitt's eyes and was replaced by a blankness. He grunted softly and then limply collapsed into the dust.

Russ shoved his gun back into its holster and stood there looking at the lifeless body before him until Edie spoke to him: "Russ! Oh no!" her young face stricken.

After that there was a crowd and confusion and Edie went back into the store with another woman, weeping brokenly, and Russ did not want to talk to Claude or to anyone. Excitement was so strong in the boy that he hopped up and down from the ground to the seat of the buckboard and back again.

Edie came out, her face red and a little mottled, not looking at Russ, and Arnold went around to her and said, "I know how you folks feel about gunfightin', but he done it for me, Edie."

Russ's face was pale and completely without expression as he climbed up into the buckboard. Edie sat far in the corner of the seat, looking straight ahead. Claude tied his horse behind as soon as the buckboard had been backed out and got up between them. The ride home was a misery, with them both strangers to him and to each other.

After he unhitched the team and put them away, Claude stood in the quiet dimness of the barn and automatically his hand fell to his gun, practicing, but he lifted it away again, shaking his head a little, the cold smoothness of the gun feeling strange and unfamiliar.

Mack Duncan came in and looked at his son and he was puzzled and wondering whether to be angry or not. He asked, "What in the devil is the matter with Edie and Russ? What'd Russ do to her?"

"Russ kilt Slick Everitt. Everitt was about to kill Arnold Hoffman over an argument an' Russ stepped in an' kilt him. Say, Pa, Russ knowed Everitt. But all he was aimin' to do was to git Arnold out of it."

He saw Pa's face harden and saw him tighten his jaw. "I knew it'd come out in him. It's good it came out now before him an' Edie—"

Pa swung around and went out of the barn. Claude had to hurry to catch up.

He cried, "Pa, don't send him away. He ain't no killer. He done it for Arnold."

Mack Duncan stopped and put a hand on the boy's shoulder. "You see why I don't like you foolin' with a gun all the time? It changes a man. He always has to wonder if he can beat somebody else. I don't want you to be like that."

Claude began, "But, Pa," wanting to explain the difference between the killer, Everitt, and Russ, but he didn't have the words.

Mack Duncan said sharply, "Don't argue now. Git some wood for your ma."

It took three loads to fill the woodbox. As he was gathering up the last armful he saw Russ go to his little room in the shed that huddled in the shelter of the barn.

Edie was helping Ma in the kitchen, her eyes red, and as Claude came in she was saying, "He looked so calm standing there, like Pa would shooting a snake or a squirrel. But it was a man he shot. Oh Ma, I guess I don't know him at all."

Pa came in and Russ followed behind and they sat down at the long table, except for Edie, who had gone to her room. Pa prayed, not quick and sloughing the words but slow, like he meant it. Then Ma put the food on the table and they set to.

Claude was ashamed for his ma and pa

31

because they were so silent and still. He was opening his mouth to speak when Russ said, "Reckon I'll jist stay the month an' then go back to Texas."

Ma looked relieved and Pa spoke, showing his shame and regret, but meeting Russ's eyes. "You been a good hand, Russ, but mebbe it's just as well." Russ knew what he meant, and so did Claude.

Claude burst out, "You ain't treatin' Russ right. He ain't done nothin' bad."

Pa glared and snapped out, "Claude!" but Claude wasn't finished. He was scared but he felt reckless too. He saw Russ shaking his head but he went on, "He saved Arnold from havin' to pull that rusty old gun an' gittin' kilt doin' it. He ain't done nothin' worse than killin' a rattler."

Mack Duncan half rose in his chair and caught Claude by his shirt front across the table. "Git up an' go to your room."

Claude left, but as he did, he saw Russ wiping his mouth and rising. Ma and Pa were left alone at the table.

Instead of going to his own room, Claude went to Edie's. She looked up as he came in, wiping tears from her eyes.

Claude said, "Pa's wrong this time. Russ

is goin' away. I hope you're satisfied." Bitterness was in his voice.

He went to the window and looked out. Russ was cantering out of the yard and his saddle and bedroll made a lumped shape on the ground beside the barn. Dusk lay over the yard, soft and heavy, and in a moment Russ was only a dark, blurred figure, growing smaller.

Claude told Edie bitterly, "Russ is leavin'. His saddle an' bedroll are there by the barn an' he's goin' after his pinto."

He heard Edie's small gasp of dismay almost lost in the squeak of the window as he forced it open. He said, "I'm goin' with him. He's no killer. I know him an' he's my friend."

He was on the ground then, outside the house, moving carefuly so as not to be seen. He got his saddle and bedroll from the barn and caught a horse out of the corral. When he heard the thundering of Russ' driven horse and, farther back, the one he rode, he was saddled, wearing his heavy coat and ready.

The pinto thundered into the corral and Russ swung down and shut the gate. Claude clambered over the corral fence and approached. Sudden shyness gripped him. He knew what he wanted to say, but did not know how to say it.

He called, "Russ!" and went over to the waiting man. "I want to go with you," and after a pause, "Kin I?"

He could not see Russ's face but he thought Russ was angry. The man's voice sounded strained.

"No. You belong here, helpin' your pa." Russ' hand laid on Claude's shoulder and gripped it. "You go with me an' you'll wind up driftin' from place to place with nothin' but a twenty-dollar horse to call your own. Stay, an' you'll be a cowman like your pa an' Arnold Hoffman. You could do worse. Your pa's a fine man."

"But I don't want to be like Pa an' Arnold. I want to be like you."

Russ's voice hardened and the boy knew he was really angry now. He rasped, "Or like Everitt maybe? No. Anyhow, what would I do with a kid taggin' along? Go on up to the house now an' let me be."

Somehow Claude could not argue with Russ like he could with Pa. He turned and went out of the corral, a smarting behind his eyes. He saw another shape running from the house and ducked into the shadow of the barn. He heard Edie's timid, breathless voice, "Russ," and the clanking of Russ's spurs as he crossed to her.

Claude could just see the dim shapes of the two of them, Russ so tall and still, Edie small beside him. He knew he had no business listening, but he couldn't make his feet move. Edie's voice came so softly that Claude could scarcely hear her.

"Russ, I'm sorry. I was wrong." Claude heard her sudden sobbing and saw the two figures merge. Edie cried, "I'll go with you if you want me."

He never heard Russ's answer if there was one. A dozen men came riding into the yard, kicking up dust that swirled before the streak of light from the open door of the house. Claude saw Pa's big shape there, and Ma's smaller, stout one.

A man called out, "Where's Russ? We come to see Russ." It was Arnold's voice.

Pa's voice was big and rough like himself. "You'll likely find him out to the barn. Come on in an' I'll send Claude after him."

Russ and Edie came away from the corral and passed Claude there in the shadows without seeing him. They were talking softly.

The men were dismounting and two of them led the horses away toward the corral.

35

Russ and Edie followed into the house and Claude tagged behind.

Arnold was talking to Pa and he said, "There's been too much trouble in town an' we've got together to ask Russ to be the marshal. Bein' easy with a gun is a trick a marshal has to have, an' with a man like Russ on the job there won't be much shootin'."

He saw Russ then, standing in the kitchen doorway. "How about it, Russ?"

Russ looked at Edie and Edie at Russ. Pa saw the look that was passing between the two. He shrugged only lightly and then he swallowed a couple of times, looking at the floor. When he looked up he was beginning to smile.

He said, " 'Pears like you'll have to ask both of them, Arnold. Looks like it might be that way now."

He laughed and Claude, who knew Pa and his way of oblique apology, grinned suddenly, letting his eyes go from Pa's face to Russ's and back again, feeling good. Edie ran to Pa, crying and laughing at the same time.

Pa said, "Reckon I couldn't see Russ for lookin' at that gun hangin' at his side."

# Massacre at Cottonwood Springs

The dust and the smell of the trail herds waiting outside of town came in on the small, hot, Kansas breeze. It made the percentage girls wrinkle their powdered noses distastefully, but it was not unpleasant to Russ Webber's nostrils. He sat, thin and ragged, on the high seat of the Conestoga wagon with his pa. The horses plodded ahead of the creaking wagon toward the center of town, and neither man nor boy saw or understood the trouble that was shaping up in front of the Mogollon Dance Palace.

Had Russ' pa been used to this sort of thing, he would have noticed the way men flattened themselves against the walls of the rough unpainted buildings, the way the group of five stood tensely alone in front of the Mogollon. He might have noticed the man across the street and the bright star that gleamed from his vest.

Russ' ma poked her head up behind them, holding the baby. She said softly and with a sort of glad relief, "This is a good place, Mark. Let's stay here."

Russ remembered now the way pa had been getting down from the wagon the last two days, sifting the soil between his bony, rough, farmer's hands. He thought of the way pa's weathered face had softened, the way the keen blue eyes had kindled. So it was no surprise when pa said, "Sure, Nellie. This is a good spot. We'll take up a place an' put down our roots. It's time."

Their progress along the street was slow, but so was the thing slow in building to a climax in front of the Mogollon. There was a campground in the grove of cottonwoods on the other side of town, and it was toward this that they were heading.

Russ saw a woman poke her head out of the store next to the Mogollon and duck back hastily, and he wondered at her sudden, startled expression that looked like fear.

All motion in this wide, dusty street seemed suspended but that of the nester's wagon, and all sound was stilled but that of its creaking wheels.

They drew abreast of the Mogollon. The stillness of the men there ceased. They moved, and these movements had the quickness of light. There was a short flurry of motion on the other side of the wagon as the lone man there headed for a doorway. Russ caught a glint of sunlight on the bit of bright metal that adorned his vest.

This was a thing that Russ could not understand, but a thing that brought fear from some deep part of him. He looked at pa's face, seeking reassurance there, but saw only pa's panicked realization that they had blundered into a crossfire. The guns appeared in the hands of the men standing in front of the Mogollon. The marshal across the street was a mere blur of motion. Pa's rough hand laid itself on Russ' back and sprawled the boy on the floorboards. One of the group of five yelled, "The marshal's gittin' away! Shoot, damn you, shoot!"

The guns belched smoke straight at the nester's wagon, seeking the man now hidden from sight behind it, and bullets tore through the wagon as it moved into their path.

There was the sound of a solid, meaty smack beside Russ and above him. Pa fell forward, dropping the reins, falling between the horses. Ma screamed. Russ lay staring stupidly, no color in his white face, his eyes wide with this quick fear.

The silence was shocking. The team nervously danced, but life, except for Russ', had ceased in the wagon.

A man stepped into the street and caught the bridle of the near horse, just as the frightened animals surged into a run. Pa's still form lay in the dusty street. Rifle fire now boomed and in quick succession, three of the gunmen in front of the Mogollon crumpled lifeless close by. The remaining two, their guns still smoking in their hands, broke into a ragged run. The rifle spoke again, and one of these stumbled and went down. The other rounded the corner beside Halliday's feed store and disappeared. The marshal stepped into the street from the doorway into which he had ducked, and crossed in the hushed silence that lay heavy and solid over this raw scene of death. He raged impotently, "Damn it, Dude got away!"

The street began to fill. Men poured from doorways all along the street. There was the sudden babble of excited talk. The marshal stirred the still figures on the board sidewalk with the toe of his boot, rifle ready. A crowd formed around the tall Conestoga wagon, and a man peering in behind cried out, "God! They got the woman . . . an' the kid!"

Another breathed, "Five men, a woman, an' a kid. Oh, Lord!"

Russ sat shocked and still on the seat. He thought wonderingly, still failing to comprehend, "A minute ago, it was all so quiet. It was all so quiet."

Folks said it was kind of funny to see the darkly handsome, powerful marshal, Jeff Thomas, walking along the street with ragged, skinny Russ Webber trailing him. They said Jeff felt guilty on account of the way the kid's folks had died. They allowed that Jeff owed the boy something, because if it hadn't been for that nester's wagon, Jeff Thomas would have been a long time dead and the town of Cottonwood Springs looking for a new marshal.

Still, nobody blamed Jeff for what had happened. He'd tried to avoid gunfire by ducking out of sight in that doorway. He'd just been a little too late.

Folks thought fourteen-year-old Russ Webber a mite queer. The boy was sullen, looking at man and woman alike out of brooding, hate-filled eyes. He slouched after Jeff Thomas like a mangy dog, its tail tucked between its legs. He got to be a kind of fixture around Cottonwood Springs that winter, and eventually the town got used to him, accepted him much as they accepted the everlasting mud in the street, the cold bite of the norther.

In April, as the marshal and the skinny, shivering boy rode through the thin slush of snow north of town, Russ asked, "Jeff, will Dude Sudler be comin' back here from Texas soon?"

For the hundredth time, Jeff answered wearily, "Reckon he will, boy. But you ain't ready for him yet. You got to practice more. You got to git faster. Dude Sudler is as mean as they come. He's fast as a sidewinder. You better let me take care of him."

They reached a spot where a wide, dry wash cut its ragged gash across the plain, and here they dismounted. Russ walked jerkily to the bank and, drawing from somewhere among his ragged garments, fired three quick shots at three white pebbles in the bank. Dust flew. He fired twice more. Two more pebbles disappeared. Jeff drawled, "You shoot mighty straight, kid, but you don't draw fast enough. If you'd let me buy you a holster . . ."

The boy shook his head, thinking of the

ridicule that was heaped upon him in the saloons and dance halls, the countless times Jeff Thomas had risked his life fighting Russ' battles. He said, "If I was to go packin' a gun in a holster, I wouldn't live long enough to kill Dude Sudler. Thisaway, ever'body thinks I'm just a ragged kid. Mostly now, they let me alone."

He reloaded the gun and fired again. He kept this up until he had shot away a full box of cartridges. Then, the oddly assorted pair mounted up and headed back to Cottonwood Springs.

Spring's warm sunshine melted the snow and dried the ground. Grass poked above it, lushly green. Flowers bloomed on the wide expanse of prairie. As the days passed, the tension began to build up in Russ. He followed the trail herds from Texas with his mind, counting each night's stop, imagining from Jeff's description of the countryside there when they crossed the Red, when they paused to pay toll to the Cherokees. He was expecting the first of the herds on the day the vanguard of them raised dust on the horizon.

But it was not the outfit of Dude Sudler, the man who had fomented the quarrel so long ago in front of the Mogollon Dance Palace. It was not the outfit of the man who had shouted as the nester's wagon drew abreast, "The marshal's gittin' away! Shoot, damn you, shoot!"

But activity in the town picked up. Marshal Jeff Thomas kept busy night-patrolling "Hide Park" and saloon row. And with him, like a shaggy, faithful dog, was always Russ Webber. Russ slouched. He shrank from attention. He kept his pale eyes on the ground. His hair was uncombed, his face unwashed. But somewhere in his tattered clothes nestled the bright, efficient Colt .45. And rankling in his heart was that wanton murder of a peaceful wagonload of settlers, his father, mother and brother.

A score of times each day he would mutter, "I'll kill him! I'll kill him! I'm good enough now. Why don't he come?"

He saw each new face in town and he kept searching. The townspeople thought him as harmless as the mayor's big shepherd dog. Pretty soon, they even stopped seeing him. He became a part of the marshal, as much a part as Jeff Thomas' twin sixguns, and not nearly so noticeable.

Dude Sudler's outfit hit Cottonwood Springs

in the late evening. In the dark, nobody saw their coming. Dude and his crew came in about eight o'clock, leaving the herd with the night guards bedded half a dozen miles outside of town.

Jeff Thomas played poker in the Green Front saloon, and Russ Webber lounged beside the door, seeming half asleep, but not missing a face that passed through it. Jeff's luck was bad. Russ could see the flush of anger mounting into the handsome face, the darkly reckless look gathering behind his eyes.

Russ knew his friend had more to drink than was good for him. He could see it in the bloodshot eyes, in the slightly unsteady hands. He watched with a kind of fascination. A town marshal of Cottonwood Springs, Kansas, had no business drinking. It slowed his hands, unsteadied his aim.

And this concern for Jeff Thomas made him miss the crowd of dusty punchers that straggled noisily through the door, Dude Sudler among them. Dude, unnoticed, laid his washed-out, merciless eyes on Russ. His thin lips lifted their corners in a mirthless grin, and he looked away, no recognition lighting his evil face. He stood an arm's length away from the kid that had sworn to kill him, and surveyed the crowd.

The marshal's eyes were on the hand he had just drawn. A scowl deepened his features. As Dude saw him, he growled, "There he is. He's been drinkin'. This ought to be easy."

Unobtrusively, he stalked through the crowd, four men behind him. In front of the marshal's table he stopped, his back to the door and to young Russ Webber. Russ still watched Jeff Thomas, only concern in his eyes.

Suddenly, Dude yelled, "You damn dirty skunk! I'm gonna blow the top of your head off!"

Russ jumped. He looked at the man, disbelief in his eyes, but still no recognition. Well, Jeff Thomas could handle this kind.

A gun leaped from the stranger's holster. Jeff Thomas started to get up. He grabbed at his holsters, but he was looking down the barrel of Dude Sudler's gun. Dude yelled again, his voice rising over the babble of loud talk, "I missed you last summer on account o' that damned nester wagon. But I won't miss this time!" Russ caught the hate in Dude's tone, wondering at its cause.

Dude fired. Blood ran redly on the marshal's throat, and the shock of the bullet knocked him back, his chair crashing. Dead silence fell over the room, broken only by the scrambling sounds of the percentage girls and customers as they dived for safety, out of the door, behind the long bar.

Dude fired again. The marshal's body jumped. The dazed look suddenly left the eyes of the boy at the door. Dude's words had given him away. Russ stepped quickly to the door, slammed it, turned the key and put it his pocket. Then, he swung around.

It was a scene that was engraved forever on his brain. Jeff Thomas lay bloody, dead on the floor beside an overturned poker table. Dude Sudler stood over him, still pumping bullets into the motionless body. Dude's villainous crew stood grinning behind him.

Now, another scene flashed brightly before Russ' eyes. A nester's wagon with a woman and child dead inside. A farmer, toil roughened but honest, kind, lying in the dusty street. And Dude Sudler running around the corner of Halliday's feed store, a smoking gun in his hand.

Somehow, the bright Colt came out of the boy's ragged garments. It leveled at Dude and began to speak. The first bullet caught Dude in the chest and he reeled away, to crash into the huddled onlookers and slump lifeless to the floor. But Russ was not finished. He couldn't quit. Guns came up in the hands of Sudler's four cronies, and the boy's Colt cracked again. Bullets whispered through the thin walls behind him. Russ had shot four times. Four men were down. The fifth had a look of sheer terror in his eyes as he turned, running, finding his way blocked by the packed crowd.

Russ' gun followed him, coughed at him, and the man went down. Someone shouted, "Gawd, shoot out the light!" The bartender's shotgun sprayed buckshot at the ceiling. The chandelier came crashing down.

The room turned black. Panic came with the darkness. Men fought, and women screamed. "Quiet, damn it! Quiet! It's all over. Git out t' the street, but take yer time!"

A badly frightened gambler fired a derringer at the door, hoping the bullet would find the murderous kid. A Texan's gun answered, and another. Women clawed toward the windows. Men cursed.

Russ unlocked the door and slipped out. The street was nearly deserted. He moved to the hitchrail and untied Jeff Thomas' horse. Mounting, he moved silently up the street and into the night. He murmured, his youthful face strangely peaceful, "Now, pa, I'll take up a place an' put down roots. It's time."

Cottonwood Springs, Kansas, never knew what became of Russ. It was assumed that he was wounded and crawled off somewhere to die. But if you were to drive your car north along the highway from Cottonwood Springs for about forty miles, you'd come to a place with a neat white house on it and a sod shack that they use for a spud cellar. It stands off to the left of the road.

If it was in the afternoon of a warm spring day, you'd probably find a peaceful old man sitting on the porch, a corncob pipe smoldering between his teeth, telling hair-raising stories to his grandchildren. Russ Webber don't look his ninety-five.

# Dobbs Ferry

Jonathan Dobbs, sweating in the blazing New Mexico sun, turned his prideful eyes from his new ferry and out across the flooding, muddy Kiowa River to watch the slow approach of a wagon on the far bank. Even at this distance, he could tell from its cobbled-up appearance and rickety progress as well as from the half-starved condition of the oxen that this would be another ferry trip for which he would receive no pay.

Unless, as his wife Charity so often insisted that he do, he refused passage on the ferry until payment was made. He shook his head stubbornly. A man set up an obligation when he put a ferry here on the trail to California—an obligation to all travelers, not just to those who had enough money for the toll. Besides, to refuse passage would be to choose among his fellow men according to their ability to pay, and he knew that possession of worldly goods was no indication of character. He would tell Charity patiently,

"I like to believe in people. Sometimes the ones least able to pay are the ones that need most to be ferried across."

A hundred yards downriver from the crossing he could see the wagon of Ute Weimer and his two companions. He wondered uneasily why they did not cross and move on. Their furtive watchfulness bothered him. He had the feeling they were counting up the tolls he collected. There in the high brush he could see a watching man's hat, the giant Kurt, he supposed, too tall to be completely concealed in the brush, too stupid to realize it.

He stepped onto the deck of the ferry bridge, a tall, gaunt man of thirty, whose stern, clean-lined face sometimes reminded travelers of a New England deacon, and took up his long pole. Fifteen minutes later, he grounded on the opposite bank. The wagon was waiting, a frowzy woman sitting patiently on the high seat, a lanky boy of fifteen beside her. The boy was just a boy, towheaded, freckled, but too thin, his eyes too old. The other, younger, sprawled in the shade of the wagon, absently flipping a knife into the ground, taking it up, flipping it again.

Mumblety-peg, thought Jonathan absently. His eyes drifted toward the wagon of Ute Weimer, toward the still-watching Kurt. The woman got down and approached, her face telling Jonathan plainly with its hesitant expression that his earlier surmise had been correct. He called, "Drive on the ferry, ma'am. Have you across in fifteen minutes. You can't ford the doggone thing this time of year unless you go fifty miles north of here." The severity of his face was broken by the kindliness and understanding that looked out of his deep-set eyes.

But the woman kept walking toward him and, when she was but a scant ten feet away, she said, her voice like the twang of a loose fiddlestring, "We can't pay, mister. I lost my man a couple of months ago. But my boys . . . maybe they can work it out."

Jonathan hated to look at her honest, pleading eyes. He didn't like to see anyone debased by having to ask for charity. He said again, more firmly now, "Drive on the ferry, ma'am. I reckon one trip for free ain't going to hurt a man."

For an instant her eyes gave him her gratitude, but then they slid away, refusing to meet his own gaze further. This momentarily upset Jonathan. He shrugged as the wagon creaked aboard. A quick glance toward Ute Weimer's camp told him he was no longer watched. He poled slowly, steadily, toward the other bank.

So many travelers along this trail were destitute nowadays, he thought. They started out full of hope for a new life in a new land, but the trail was too long and too hard for many of them. To the west of here the bones of their animals bleached beside the trail. Here and there a frail cross marked a solitary grave. Charity often said to Jonathan, "It would be a greater kindness if you'd refuse to take 'em across, Jonathan. Then maybe they'd go home and stay alive."

Yet even with all those Jonathan passed free, the ferry was paying handsomely. Maybe even enough to tempt Ute Weimer's sort, he reflected, and thought fleetingly about Charity's insistence that he carry a gun. She might be right in that. It was lonely out here, with no law save for what a man made for himself.

The woman volunteered, "I'm Beulah Neely, mister. The oldest boy here is Jess an' the other's Mark. They're good workers. What would you like for 'em to do?"

Jonathan laughed. "Why ma'am, I don't reckon there's anything here that needs doin' very bad. Besides, there's a wagon train a couple of hours ahead of you. If you was to hurry, you could catch 'em yet tonight. Then you wouldn't have to travel all alone."

As he neared the western bank, he could see the curtains in their sod house pulled aside and a hint of Charity's sharp face in the window. He was a little disturbed sometimes by Charity's hardness and lack of generosity. He thought now, "She ain't naturally that way at all. It's just a quirk in her that makes her figure if she don't look out for herself, nobody else will." He grinned ruefully to himself, thinking, "Ute Weimer watches me on one bank and Charity on the other. Reckon I ain't got much chance for wrongdoin', even I was inclined that way."

He watched the Neelys drive off the ferry and away and waved to them, embarrassed by their thanks, which had somehow seemed a little forced and not as straightforward as they might have been. But their friendship made him feel warm. No traveler, paying or otherwise, ever continued west without feeling friendship for Jonathan. He was that kind of man. There was a bigness of heart to him that attracted men and women, young and old alike. He sometimes told Charity, "A kindness is like a coin, because it seems like a body gettin' it can't wait to turn around and spend it on someone else."

He watched the wagon creaking laboriously westward for a moment, then braced himself and went inside, as ready now as he would ever be for Charity's sharp upbraiding, her scolding tongue.

She did not disappoint him. As he entered the dim shanty, she said sharply, "You crossed 'em for free, didn't you? I can tell by the looks of you whether you get paid or not. When you goin' to learn . . . ?"

He wished he could change her in this, could make her see. She was so generous underneath, if only she'd let it come out and not be so afraid. A hail from across the river halted her tirade and as Jonathan turned to go outside, she scolded, "Now you see you get paid for this one, you hear? A body gets tired of seeing you pass 'em without paying, and us needing things here for the house and all." He didn't answer and she shrilled, "You hear me, Jonathan? You see you get paid for this one!"

He felt the stirring of mutiny in him, felt his anger rise. He growled impatiently, "All right, all right! I'll get paid for this one. I promise you!"

He went down to the riverbank. He could

see the wagon of Ute Weimer waiting on the other side. He'd soon know their intentions, he thought. Nervousness built up in his body. He thought of going back to the house for his gun, then put the impulse aside. At least he could make good on his promise to Charity without working a hardship on any-one.

He poled the barge across, letting his eyes wander out across the limitless expanse of rolling grassland dotted with cedars and sagebrush, along the river lined with willows and cottonwoods. It gave him a feeling of insignificance. The sun hung low in the west, like a ball of molten gold.

Nearing the other bank, he saw Ute Weimer and the man they called Slasher waiting on the ground. The giant Kurt sat on the wagon seat. It had seemed strange to Jonathan four days ago to see their kind riding in a wagon. They seemed more the type to travel horseback. He had done some speculating about this, but eventually had shrugged off his thoughts as foolishness.

Ute had a face like a hawk, a hooked sharp nose and beady bright eyes above. His skin was like an old harness leather, gray with age and dust, cracked and wrinkled from exposure to the weather.

Slasher was a slim young man who carried a broad-knife in a scabbard at the back of his belt and no other weapon. Kurt was a monstrous man, powerfully muscled and obviously very strong. Yet Kurt's face was singularly blank of expression and his eyes were vacant and dumb. It was Kurt who did all the heavy work around the camp, obeying the orders of Ute and Slasher dumbly and unquestioningly.

The barge grounded. Kurt whipped up the horses and the wagon rolled onto the ferry barge. Ute and Slasher walked aboard and Ute grinned at Jonathan as he said, "Busy here, ain't you? Take in a sizable piece of money every day. We been watchin' you."

Jonathan's feeling of uneasiness came back, as if he could read in the thoughts of these men that they meant him harm. He wished suddenly that he hadn't scoffed at Charity's suggestion that he carry a gun. But he forced his nervousness away, thinking, "A man makes up troubles in his mind. That's all it is."

He nodded to Ute. "Yep. Been runnin' a little over a month now and I can't complain. Freighted the ferry here from St.

Louis. Been nearly six months putting her together and getting her afloat."

Ute and Slasher went over to the far side of the barge behind the bulk of the wagon. He could hear the murmur of their whispered talk over the rushing small sound of water slapping against the barge's side. Out of all of it, though, he only made out one sentence, spoken to the giant on the wagon seat, "Kurt, you watch the team."

He poled stolidly, steadily. He kept telling himself that this was only another crossing, like a hundred others before, that as soon as they reached the far bank, Ute Weimer and the others would drive on. But Charity's worried voice kept coming back to him. "I don't like the looks of that bunch, Jonathan. They're trashy and no good. You take your gun and carry it. Show 'em you ain't helpless, and maybe they'll move on."

That had been two nights ago, when Charity had ridden across on the ferry with him, "just to get out of that stuffy house for a while."

She had asked, "Why do they keep watchin' us all the time?" when she had seen Kurt half hidden in the brush. The surveillance had bothered Jonathan, too, but he hoped it was over now. He hoped Ute and his friends would drive on west tonight and there would be nothing more to worry about. The ferry grounded and Kurt drove the wagon off. He stopped and Jonathan said, "That'll be three dollars, one for each of you."

Ute and Slasher came forward as Jonathan was tying up the barge. "Reckon we could borrow a bit of salt from you?"

Jonathan nodded shortly and led the way to the shanty. He opened the door. Charity's shrill cry was the first inkling he had that all was not well behind him. Ute Weimer had a gun in his hand and Slasher's knife was out, naked and gleaming in the last rays of the sun. Ute growled, "Don't make no sudden moves. We've just decided to take over the ferry." He shoved Jonathan aside and went into the shanty, pushing Charity roughly back. She stumbled and nearly fell.

Jonathan forgot their weapons in his sudden rage at this. He lunged at Ute, knocking the man to the floor with a single blow of his bony fist. The gun went sliding across the packed, clean-swept earth floor. Charity screamed, "Jonathan! The knife!"

Turning, Jonathan arched his body. Slasher drove past him, falling, and the knife buried itself in the floor to the hilt.

Jonathan kicked viciously. His booted foot made a crushing sound as it connected with Slasher's jaw. Blood welled out, the man lay still. Ute was up and had recovered the gun. He raised it, his sharp face cold and deadly. Jonathan, ten feet away, watched the gaping muzzle, the tightening trigger finger with fascination.

Then something flashed between him and Ute—something bright. It was Charity in her gingham dress. Jonathan leaped forward, crashed into her and knocked her sprawling to the floor. The gun cracked, but both Jonathan and his wife were down now and he covered her with his body, waiting, waiting for the pistol's second report.

The shot never came. Kurt came stooping through the door and Ute holstered the gun, still cursing softly. He growled, "He might look like a damn church deacon but, by God, he can scrap." He seemed to hold no animosity for the blow Jonathan had struck him or for Slasher's broken jaw.

Slasher was not so generous. He raised up, jaw hanging loose, face contorted with pain. He recovered the knife and stood wiping the blade on his pants, watching Jonathan steadily in much the same way a hungry cougar might watch a frightened colt.

Ute spoke to Charity, "Stir up some grub."

Jonathan could see nothing but death ahead for the two of them. Ute couldn't release them; he couldn't let them go. He'd have to kill them if he intended to take over the ferry. And that was what he'd said he meant to do.

He helped Charity to her feet. Ute made him hold his hands out in front of him and then tied them with a length of rope. Jonathan supposed Ute had tied his hands in front so that he wouldn't have to untie them for him to eat. Ute pushed him toward the bed and he sat on the edge of it while Charity prepared supper. Slasher sat down on the one chair facing him, knife out hopefully.

Charity dropped a pot of stew in her nervousness and Ute cursed her. Jonathan scowled up at him, wanting to close Ute's mouth with his fist, knowing if he tried Slasher would open him up like a sack of grain. He'd be no help to Charity if Slasher took to him with that knife.

Soft dusk lay outside the shanty by the time Charity laid out the meal on the rude table. Ute and Kurt lined up alongside it and sat on the bench. Slasher stayed where he was, occasionally looking over his shoulder at the food, licking his lips, his face gray with pain. Jonathan felt no hunger, only hopelessness. There was no help for them now. Nobody would be coming to cross the river at night and by tomorrow. . . .

Pleading now, the fight gone from his voice, he said, "I reckon I know what you figure to do with us, an' I guess it'll have to be all right for me. But for the love of God, let Charity go!"

Slasher chuckled, then stopped as his jaw pained from the movement of his laugh.

Jonathan held his temper. Furtively, his eyes swept the cabin. If a man was going to die, he'd feel better about it if he died trying, fighting, doing something. If he only had something to hold in his two bound hands. But nothing was within his reach.

It kind of made a man wonder, after all his talking about how decent people were and how it paid to do folks little kindnesses, to face dying like this. He guessed that now he could understand Charity better, her philosophy of, "Devil take the hindmost. If you don't look out for yourself, it's sure nobody else will." Maybe there was some logic in her ideas.

With sudden surprise he thought, "Maybe

this is the kind of folks Charity's seen the most of. With me, it's the other way around. I ain't seen many like these three. Maybe that's why Charity and me don't see eye-to-eye."

Speaking carefully because of his jaw and sounding as though he had a mouthful of mush, Slasher said, "Ute, what the hell you waitin' for? Lemme take this jigger out an'. . . ."

Charity screamed, "You let Jonathan alone! You . . . !"

Her scream covered what Jonathan thought was a slight sound outside the open door. Hope boiled up in him, but the sound was not repeated and he decided he had imagined it. Then he heard a small, weak thud, and this sound was inside the cabin and unmistakable. Ute, sitting at the table wolfing the food Charity had intended for Jonathan's supper tonight, grunted explosively. Jonathan stared at him in surprise. Something whizzed through the air in front of his eyes and Ute yelled, getting up and falling backward over the bench.

Jonathan continued to stare at him, unbelieving. Ute rolled on the floor, choking and gasping. Kurt still sat at the table, looking stupidly and uncomprehendingly at the man thrashing around on the floor. Jonathan said silently, "Mumblety-peg."

Surprised at his own quick thinking, he flung himself backward on the bed, bringing his feet up, doubling his knees against his belly. He roared, "Ouch! Oh, Lordy, something hit me in the belly!"

Slasher looked at him murderously, sure that somehow Jonathan was responsible for the pain Ute was in. He got up and moved toward Jonathan, knife held ready in his hand. When he was close enough, Jonathan straightened his legs, kicking with both feet. He caught Slasher in the chest. The breath went out of the man with an explosive grunt. The knife flew into the air and Jonathan caught it coming down, but by the blade.

He felt the sharpness cut his hand to the bone, but he flipped it back into the air and this time caught it by the handle as it came down. He flung it at Kurt, who was dumbly trying to bring his gun to bear. The gun went off but the bullet caught Slasher, just rising in front of Jonathan, in the back of the head.

The heavy-bladed knife hit Kurt in the face, not cutting him but making him throw up his hands protectively. Jonathan hurdled the falling body of Slasher, and his hands, still bound and bleeding profusely from the knife, caught at the gun and wrenched it from Kurt's momentarily light grasp. Jumping back, Jonathan bawled "Get back! Get back or I'll shoot."

Kurt, great, stupid hulk that he was, knowing his two masters were dead, kept coming, his lips drawn from his teeth. He was a big, grizzly bear of a man who would not stop now until he had torn Jonathan to pieces or until he was dead. He pawed at Jonathan, cuffing at him the way a grizzly might, but Jonathan kept backing until at last the wall was at his back. Then he fired, reluctantly, again and again, ducking sideways at the last minute to avoid the great hands trying to come to grips with him. Kurt went down, dying slowly and reluctantly.

Through all of this, an accompaniment to his action, Jonathan had heard the steady screaming of Charity and he had kept hoping she would stay out of it. When he was able to look for her, he saw that she stood holding a rifle, swinging the muzzle back and forth wildly, her eyes terrified, wanting to shoot but afraid of hitting Jonathan. He said, "Put it down, Charity. It's over now."

Kurt lay still on the floor and the land

outside the door lay gray and bleak and empty. Jonathan yelled, "All right, boys! You can come in now!"

Jess Neely appeared in the doorway and behind him, Mark. Both were pale and trembling. Jess quavered worriedly, "Did we do right?"

"Well now, I'll say you did. Nobody could have done better, that's for sure."

Charity began, "What . . . ?" and Jonathan answered her. "Mumblety-peg. It's a game kids play when they throw a knife and stick it in the ground. Only tonight these kids stuck their knives in Ute's back instead of the ground."

Charity cut the ropes on his wrists and bound up his cut hand. Then, with the assistance of the boys, he dragged out the bodies of the outlaws and laid them side by side ready for burial tomorrow.

Back inside, he asked young Jess, "What in tarnation made you come back?"

The older boy put a grubby hand deep into the pocket of his ragged pants. It came out clutching three silver dollars. He said haltingly, "Ma . . . well, Ma wasn't quite tellin' the truth when she said we couldn't pay. I reckon she meant to say that we couldn't hardly pay. She wanted Mark and me to work for you and save this for maybe later when we'd need it bad."

Jonathan felt a surge of renewed faith and asked, "But how'd you happen to come back?"

"Well, Ma kept feelin' meaner an' meaner about not payin' you. Purty soon she just couldn't stand it no more. She stopped the wagon an' told us to get on back here an' give you the money. We sneaked up . . ." the boy's face colored with embarrassment but he went gamely on . . . "playin' Injuns, an' when we seen somethin' was wrong, why, we listened, that's all. Soon's we knew what was wrong . . . well, we just tried to help."

Jonathan grinned at Charity. He stuck out his hand. The boy put the three dollars into it. Charity gasped, "No, Jonathan!"

Jonathan's grin widened wickedly. "Yep. We got to get paid. You said so yourself."

Charity looked at him as though he were a stranger. Jonathan said, "We owe you fellers somethin' too, though. After all, you kind of saved our necks." He scratched his head, trying to keep his face solemn and straight. "I got it," he said at last. "That wagon and them horses of Ute's. Those fellers ain't got use for 'em no more. You boys take the wagon and go catch up with your ma."

He had an arm around his wife's slim waist as they watched the wagon fade into the darkness. The starlight showed a softness in Charity's face Jonathan had never seen in it before. Did a woman good to be fought for, he thought. Did a woman good to know other folks cared enough to help her, too. He said, "Doggone it, you told me to be sure an' get paid for bringing Ute and them other two across. And I let that wagon go. . . ."

No sharpness, only a shy sort of shame was in her voice as she answered him. "You can quit scolding me, Jonathan. Those boys showed me how wrong I've been."

Jonathan felt warm inside as he walked her back to the shanty. He tightened his arm around her waist and suddenly she giggled, snuggling closer like a girl.

# High-Carded

George Sexton stood up impatiently, "Daggone it, Wesley, I don't need you to tell me what I have to do. If I resign you'll have to hoist your fat carcass onto that sway-backed mare an' go after him yourself."

He felt a stirring of disgust as he looked at Sheriff Wesley Terry, whose big body spread to fill the swivel chair like gelatin in a bowl. He took his gun belt down from a nail and strapped it on. He hesitated over the deputy's badge, then unpinned it and slipped it into his pocket. "Cade will know I'm after him without parading this. No use to rub it in."

As he rode down Main and out of town he kept ignoring the gnawing at the back of his mind, as though by his refusal to recognize the fear he could eliminate it. But he could read the question in everyone's eyes as they furtively glanced at his set, bitter face: What if he won't come in? What if he says, "Go to hell, George. Come and get me."

George knew they'd be laying bets on that down in the Stockmen's & Farmers' Saloon. He wondered what the odds would be. He could almost hear the talk.

"Two to one he'll bring Cade in alive. Cade's too blamed used to losin' to George to put up much of a fight."

"Cade hates the air George breathes. He'll fight, but I reckon he won't have much chance agin' George."

George scowled. A man lived by a certain set of values and it gained him nothing to doubt them. Pa had always said, "Idea is to win—to come out on top. A winner is what folks respect in this world."

Suddenly George hated the townspeople. Pity for him in this predicament, or understanding, he saw in not one face—only the avid, waiting tenseness, their eyes dilated with expectancy.

They'd all wanted to form a posse and go along, but George had been firm about this. Too many accidents could happen when a bunch of townsmen went on a manhunt. He'd told the sheriff, "I'm hanged if I'll head up a posse. If you figure it's going to take more than one man, go get him yourself!" George well knew the sheriff had no intention of exposing himself either to the saddle or to hostile gunfire.

Wasn't much doubt where Cade would be. He'd been wounded and would have to head somewhere where he could rest up and heal. That would be the old Hollister homestead shack where as boys they'd gone on overnight pack trips whenever their father, old Luther Sexton, would let them off long enough from the ranch work in summer.

So George took the trail up Red Creek, staying high, out of the willow tangle in the bottom, but looking down at the tumbling, white water. He had fished with Cade in Red Creek when they were kids, before . . . well, a long time ago. Down there was a bend, a deep pool where he'd caught "Old Mossyhorns," the largest trout ever to come out of Red Creek.

Recalling that big fish set him to thinking. Cade had been awful sure that he, and not George, would get "Old Mossyhorns." Cade had hooked the monster three times, lost him all three. And Luther, hearing his two sons talking one day, offered the one that caught the fish a new Colt six-shooter. Pa was always doing that, George remembered. Pitting one against the other. Maybe that was most of the trouble—the trouble that came later. The spirit of competition was too strongly developed.

George's hand dropped unconsciously, caressing the worn grips of the Colt at his side. The same gun. He'd carried it all these years. Come to think of it, the thing must have been a constant source of irritation to Cade—a sort of symbol of failure. Because Cade had gotten an old one, one the foreman gave him, and somehow never quite came up to George's markmanship with it.

It really went back further even than the fish. But the fish and the gun had been the beginning of the bitterness in Cade, and he had begun to blame George for his failures—George who couldn't lose at anything, who took each victory as though it was his due. George wondered why a realization as important as this one always came to a man too late.

George had been ten when he caught "Old Mossyhorns." Cade nine. Some way, old Luther Sexton thought continual striving would make better men of them both. Trouble was, George had always possessed just a little bit more persistence, a little more confidence, a tiny bit more ability—or possibly it was just his age. Too, George favored

Luther, Cade his mother who had died bearing him, and maybe that accounted for the difference.

The small victories had been George's all along the line, but they had not seemed small at the time. And failure, continual, inevitable, had gradually begun to warp Cade's character.

The sun climbed in the sky and heat waves shimmered from the parched ground. "Funny," thought George, "how everything a man sees reminds him of somethin'."

There was the old corral, gray, weathered, mostly rotten and falling to the ground. It kind of marked the second important episode in the shaping of two lives.

Wild horses. That was the year the cavalry was calling for remounts. George was fifteen that year. Cattle were cheap. Luther figured if he could corral a couple of hundred wild horses, cull them and break the best of the lot, he could make some money selling remounts. Looking back at the incident, George's face suddenly felt hot and he was not very proud. He hadn't really meant it to turn out that way, and Pa's making such a to-do over it had just made it worse.

George let his horse have its head and,

chin sunk to his chest, his eyes turned blank and faraway.

Pa stationed George and Cade, one at the end of each corral wing, back far enough in the high brush to be hidden from sight, with instructions to ride in as soon as the wild horses ran into the corral and block the entrance until the rest of the crew could arrive and put up the poles.

Suspense tingled through George, waiting. Then horses, a hundred head or more, thundered down the valley, leaping washes, hammering through the brush, beating it to the ground. Dust rose in acrid, choking clouds from their frantic hooves. Their sides gleamed with sweat.

Young George trembled with anticipation. "Go on in, you devils!" he whispered hoarsely as they slowed in front of the corral, went to milling. "Go on in!"

He glanced across the valley, looking for Cade, but his brother was invisible in the tall brush.

Half a mile away, Luther and the rest of the crew, knowing that the horses would now be very near the corral, released a volley of shots, a wild chorus of yells.

"Attaboy, Pop," said George softly, and watched the horses resume their slow forward movement into the corral. Half a dozen were still outside when he spurred his mount, thundered out of hiding and down toward the open gate. But Cade was ahead of him, riding like crazy, yelling like a Comanche.

George muttered, "You crazy fool! You'll pull them all out, yelling like that. Take it easy!"

Cade reached the opening, leaped from his horse. He stood in the gate, waving his arms, yelling. George bawled, "Shut up, blame you! You'll scare them crazy an' they'll rush you!"

Bitter had been Cade's eyes, looking up, bitter his words. "Got to be first at everything, don't you, George? Can't stand to be beat."

Funny. George hadn't even been beat that time. He was still fifty feet away when a big sorrel stallion screamed, pawed, and rushed Cade, the whole bunch behind him.

Cade stood for a moment, whitening, his eyes wide and staring. Then his nerve broke and he abandoned his post, scrambling for the wing. George, who had thought his presence beside Cade might stop the stallion and who had already dismounted, found himself suddenly alone, thirty feet in front of the maddened beast.

Sheer terror overwhelmed him momentarily, froze him in his tracks. An awesome sight, that stallion thundering down on him. It would have been no disgrace for a boy to run, but George couldn't do it. Cade had run and George figured he was better than Cade. George pulled the Colt six-shooter and dropped the stallion, and the shot turned the rest of them back. Luther and the crew rode up just in time to see the whole thing.

Looking back on it now, George wondered why he hadn't told Cade and the rest of them how scared he was. It might have helped. It might have dulled the flame of hate that kindled in Cade's eyes. It might even have kept unsaid the puncher's comment, muttered but heard by them both, "George's got twice the guts the young one has."

Water under the bridge. If any one of the episodes George could remember had been reversed, if Cade had ever won a really important victory over him, the whole course of their lives might have been changed.

He came to the place where the trail forked, took the right turn. Rising now, he could look back down the valley into hazy distance.

It was hard to believe, Cade Sexton wanted for attempted train robbery, the only survivor of the crew that made the abortive attempt. Cade Sexton, running, hiding, pursued by his own brother, the deputy sheriff, sworn to uphold the law. Cade, dark of hair, slim, laughing of eye in those early years, lately grown moody and sullen.

Down there, almost out of sight in the haze that lay over the valley, was the McCollum's place. George thought of Jenny McCollum, and Jenny was another link in the chain of unfortunate events.

It made a man sick, looking back on it all like this. Of what good to him now was the fact he had always bested Cade? Why couldn't he have seen it as clearly, going along, as he did now? Things might have been so different.

Luther was aging, failing, the year the McCollums moved into the valley. Most of the ranch work was falling on George, who seemed naturally to assume it, and he and Cade, formerly so close, were virtual strangers.

Jenny was a pretty, empty-headed little thing, her eyes perhaps a shade too calculating, her red mouth too likely to pout if she did not always get her own way.

But with women as scarce as they were, the punchers that hung around the McCollums' sod-roofed shack were not inclined to be too particular.

Cade went all out for Jenny. And Jenny, wise enough to weigh the size and richness of Luther Sexton's Square S outfit against the empty jeans of the drifting punchers, soon ran off everybody but Cade—and, of course, George.

The worst part of that deal, George reflected, was that he hadn't even wanted Jenny. Maybe he'd seen through her. Maybe he'd been too tired from overwork to react to her the way a healthy man should. His only visits to the McCollum place had been on business, and he'd had nothing whatever to do with what happened. But could Cade see that? Hell no! Not Cade with a chip on his shoulder.

George always suspected that what happened was Luther's last blundering act of building, stone upon stone, the wall that now stood between George and Cade. George figured Luther had gone that day and seen Jenny, maybe told her that George and not Cade would inherit the Square S. Luther must have known George was not interested in Jenny. He'd probably wanted to free Cade of her.

Telling Jenny that would have made a difference, all right, Jenny being what she was. And Cade was better off for being turned down by her. "It's George I love, Cade, dear. I can't help myself. I worship the ground he walks on." Sure she did, thought George, as long as it was Square S ground.

Blunders, mistakes, things misunderstood. Well, Jenny was gone, the sod-roofed shack only a cattle shelter now. The fish, "Old Mossyhorns," had long ago been eaten. The remount horses were smooth-mouthed now and out to pasture—or dead. But all had marked Cade's character, and George's, and the marks remained. Now was left only the final act of indignity, for Cade to be captured or killed by his brother George.

The trail entered rimrock, wound back and forth half a dozen times, and came out on top of the butte. George rode unseeingly, engrossed in his memories of days gone by.

Luther had been gone five years when the panic struck, and blackleg hit Square S at the same time. George had been for tightening up, letting most of the hands go, trying to weather it. But Cade had advised in his belligerent way, "Hell, don't be a sissy, George! Go borrow some money, replace what we've lost and keep building. That's what the Old Man would have done."

And that's what George did, mostly because he didn't want to drive Cade any further away from him, because he was older now and beginning to see just how petty those small triumphs were. When it was finished they'd both gone broke and the Square S was divided up and sold to a score of newcomers to the country. But Cade's hate had been kindled anew, because George had been right, as usual.

"About a mile, now," muttered George. "Another thirty minutes and it will be all over."

Autumn's early frost had colored the quakie leaves, had turned the long grass underfoot a dusty color. A deer bounded out of the trail, unnoticed. A breeze came whispering down off the heights, a cool breeze, full of the promise of winter.

How fast time went. It seemed only yesterday that George had accepted the deputy's job, but actually it had been almost a year. Cade had spent it hanging around the Stockmen's & Farmers' Saloon, cementing acquaintances formed through the years, acquaintances he could feel equal, even superior to. A year of working only when necessary, quitting as soon as he had a month's pay. For, quick as the Square S had gone out of their hands, Cade had dropped George like a bob-tailed flush, rejecting coldly all George's overtures.

George moved off the trail, down through the quakies toward the old Hollister homestead cabin. "I'll ride in openly," he told himself. "Cade wouldn't shoot without warnin'."

In his mind was a good picture of the shack, weeds and grass growing in profusion from its sod roof, half buried back in the side of the hill for warmth, its pole rafters extending in front to form a porch. "Bet it's gone to rot since I seen it last."

He would come out of the timber a hundred yards from the shack, the way he and Cade had come up on the place a hundred times together when they were kids.

In his memory the shack was a place of comradeship with Cade. A place of boyish dreams, a place where shrill yells echoed, where childish Indians and outlaws ran rampant. It was a place where charred steak and potatoes tasted better than anything they ever had at home, where rivalry and bitterness could be forgotten—at least in the beginning.

Impatiently he shook his head. A man took an oath and he was expected to live up to it. George rode into the clearing and there was Cade, a rifle in his hands.

George beat down the impulse to check his horse. He kept going, looking quietly at Cade, hoping desperately the kid wouldn't get panicked and do something foolish. Cade wasn't a kid any more. He was nearing thirty.

"I figured you'd be here," George said.

Cade's lip curled. "You're always figurin', an' you're always right, ain't you? Well, I won't be high-carded this time, George. If you take me back, I'll be dead when you do it!"

There was no use explaining to the hate in Cade's eyes that he'd taken an oath to uphold the law. There was no use explaining anything.

His hand and arm muscles tensed. This was an end to rivalry. Could old Luther have seen it years ago when he began to build up the thing between his sons? No. No man can see twenty-five years into the future. If he could he wouldn't make so many mistakes.

Cade's eyes narrowed, his knuckles showed white against the brown stock and blued barrel of the rifle. George waited.

Cade's nerve broke first. "Judge, jury and executioner!" he screamed. "God himself, ain't you? Funny as it sounds, you was always God to me." The man was almost sobbing now. "I thought the sun rose and set on you when we was kids an' came up here. But you always had to be showin' Pa and the rest of the country that you was better than me. Now you come up here with that gun Pa gave you hangin' at your side to show everybody one last time. Well, get on with it! No use standin' here all day!" He moved the rifle muzzle ever so slightly.

For a moment, George made no move. Then, dumbly, he shook his head. His shoulders sagged. Slowly, his hand went to his vest pocket, withdrew the deputy's badge, and tossed it at Cade's feet. "You got more to fight for than I have, Cade. I reckon I can't beat you this time."

Cade looked surprised. He had never seen weakness in George before. Then George saw something in his brother's face, too, he'd never seen there before.

Cade asked incredulously, "You mean you ain't going to try an' take me in?"

George shook his head, "Pa had you an' me workin' against each other all our lives, when he should have had us workin' together. We're through with that. Go where you want. I'll ride the other way."

Cade looked long and hard at George. "No," he said slowly, new strength and confidence in his voice. "No, I think I'll just go in an' give myself up." He turned abruptly to his tethered horse.

George watched him ride into the timber. George didn't know what to think hardly. Why did a man have to be thirty years old before he got any sense? If he'd done something like this years ago. . . . He yelled, "There's a place in Arizona called Tombstone—mining town. I'll be there waitin'."

No answer came out of the timber, but he knew Cade had heard. And he guessed he knew Cade would come.

# Nester Kid

A showdown was long overdue in the Granite Peaks valley. Squint Mooney showed a seamed and worried countenance and a pair of shrewd, narrowed eyes to the assembled cowmen at the Association meeting in the big dining-room of the Longhorn Hotel.

"That damned Pollock kid is doin' somethin' out on the flat that no nester's been able to do before. He's raisin' wheat. The weather's been just right, an' if the damned stuff makes, there'll be hell to pay. Crop failures is all that's been keepin' this country from bein' settled solid. We better do somethin', boys. If we let this kid's crops mature we're finished. They'll fence that creek in solid an' then where'll the cattle drink? We'll lose a strip of grass five miles deep along both sides of the creek."

Squint was a man without too many friends. He was quarrelsome, too ready with his gun, and he was strongly suspected of a lot of quiet brand changing at which he had so far been too smart to get caught. A lot of folks thought that his M Spear herd increased a little too fast. But now, in this matter of the nester family, he had a substantial backing.

Gus Altman got to his feet, a tall, solid man, quiet of face but with determination in his gray eyes and in the grim set of his mouth. He shouted, beating down the babble of voices:

"Squint says do somethin'. Don't know what the hell you can do. Can't run that little kid an' his maw an' them two babies out like you would a man. That kid don't look like the kind to run easy. Might try buyin' him out—if he'd sell, but I got a notion he sets a heap of store by that little chunk o' ground."

"The hell we can't run 'em out!" This was Squint again, angered as always by any opposition. "By God, it's run 'em out or git run out ourselves. Take your pick, boys!"

Gus's tone was soft, but it had a quality to it that made Squint glance sharply at him. "You ain't very solid in this country, if a twelve-year-old kid can run you out. My A Bar outfit will have no part in bullyin' that kid. There's been too damned much of that. Some of you boys remember the last nester that was run out—Frank Eckert."

In his mind was a picture of that sorry spectacle, the man dead on the ground, a half-drawn gun gripped in his hand, a weeping woman crouching beside him, cursing cows and cowmen and cow country. Gus would never forget the two little kids, dazed and sobbing with fear. He would never stop blaming himself because he hadn't stopped it. It had just happened too fast.

When Frank Eckert's wife had left, she had carried with her a sizable amount of Gus Altman's cash, and although he knew this could not pay her for the loss of her man's life or lift from him his burden of guilt, still it had made her trip easier, it had assured the necessities to the woman and her children until they reached her family in Missouri.

In the end, the meeting was split two ways, one faction siding with Squint Mooney, the other with Gus. Squint's faction adjourned to the Excelsior saloon, muttering and plainly planning something.

Gus climbed into his buckboard and drove toward home. Three miles out he passed the quarter section of land that the Pollocks occupied, operated since spring by Ernie

Pollock, a thin twelve-year-old. Jasper Pollock, the boy's father, had been killed last year by a runaway team, plowing the very land on which wheat now waved in the hot wind, a deep green, but growing fast and beginning to head out.

The kid, Ernie, was out plowing, getting ready to summer-fallow another forty this year. *That's the secret of it,* Gus mused. *Summer-fallow the land an' raise your crop with last year's moisture. That's what none of the others have been able to figure out.*

Gus watched the boy fight the heavy walking-plow a hundred yards and rest, fight it for another hundred yards before he rode out of sight into the cottonwoods that lined the creek. Admiration for the kid's persistence stirred in Gus. And the picture of the other nester, Eckert, dead on the ground, was an uneasy shadow in his memory.

Full of vague unease, he drove the remaining twelve miles to the log-and-shake ranch house that he himself had built fifteen years ago. That had been tough, too. He'd had to fight the big, entrenched cowmen then himself, in much the same way that the nesters now fought all cattlemen. This memory gave him a sort of reluctant sympathy for the nesters. Besides, the problem wasn't as serious as Squint claimed. The cattlemen could file homestead claims at intervals along the creek and leave them open to the water.

Carol, his wife, waved to him as he passed through the yard on the way to the corral. Resolutely, Gus shook the dark thoughts from his head, unhitched the team from the buckboard, and threw them down a couple of forkfuls of hay.

Squint Mooney raised his glass in the Excelsior and downed the fiery liquor at a gulp, grimacing afterward, but feeling the coursing warmth in his throat and stomach.

He shouted, "If the rest of you ain't got the guts to back me up, then by God I'll do it myself. It didn't used to be that you was all so damned squeamish. Most of you was along when that damned stubborn jackass, Eckert, was killed a couple of years ago. What in hell's the difference now? You fellers figured there was plenty of danger when Eckert settled along the creek. This is worse. It's bad enough to have these homesteaders comin' an' goin' all the time, but when they start raisin' crops an' lookin' like they was goin' to stay, then by God it's time to put a stop to it!"

Squint's bullet was the one that had cut Eckert down, but that was a thing he kept to himself, knowing in an obscure, instinctive way, that while men may condone killing they invariably feel revulsion toward the killer.

There was a twisted something in Squint Mooney's nature that made the persecution of nesters give him a sort of sadistic pleasure. And if they wouldn't fight, wouldn't even argue with him, he always gave them cause to fight, thereafter beating them insensible with his huge fists. Of course this boy wouldn't be much fun, but maybe he could rig it up in such a way that—

"What you gonna do, Squint?" asked a man at his elbow.

"Why, I reckon it'd be a good idea to cut the kid's fence. Then we kin shove forty, fifty of my M Spear steers in on that wheat. In the mornin' when the kid gets up—" He laughed harshly. "What would you do in a situation like that, Bill?"

"I bet I'd shoot me a steer." A wide grin spread across Bill Casway's face. "I git you, Squint. You aim to be there in the mornin'. You figure mebbe somethin' like that might be fun."

Half a dozen of the men in the saloon

laughed uproariously. The rest, some fifteen of them, drifted out of the doors, faces hard and showing the same revulsion a man feels watching a cat play with a chipmunk.

Night came, soft and black and starless over the land. Ernie Pollock slept in a dead coma of exhaustion. Gus Altman lay long awake, still with the uneasy image of Eckert in his mind, and the memory of Ernie Pollock, plowing and resting, plowing again, a small determined figure in afternoon's blazing heat.

His wife stirred beside him, asking, "What's the matter tonight, Gus? Can't you sleep?"

"We'll get up early in the morning," he answered. "I've got a long ride to make before sunup." And he thought to himself, *Mebbe I can do somethin' tomorrow to even up for Eckert,* promptly sleeping with this thought turning comfortably in his head.

This morning, as every morning, young Ernie Pollock awoke at five and lay motionless in his hard bed, feeling the ache in his muscles, and at this time of day, a sort of hopelessness and the crowding desire to just up and quit trying. Feeling this, he always leaped out of bed, spending this early hour in building up the fire for his ma, fetching in wood, milking the lone cow that stood placidly in the small wire corral.

Responsibility lay heavily on his narrow shoulders. It turned him quiet of face, put a brooding defiance into his twelve-year-old eyes, as though he were saying to this harsh land and to its harsh inhabitants. *I'm a grown man now. I got to be a man now that Pa's gone. I'll show you!*

But the endless heavy work of spring had put a ceaseless soreness into his thin, stringy body. And every time a bunch of punchers rode past on the way to town, Ernie shivered wordlessly until they were safely past. It was the old, old story of a sodbuster's family and a cattle country. Of fences against open range. Of peaceful men of the land against hard-riding, hard-fighting men of the saddle.

Carrying the milk back to the house, a thin smile played across his sun-reddened face as he thought of the wheat, even now a thick green coverlet across the south field, starting already to head out. Pa had plowed most of the field last spring before he died, but Ernie himself had finished, summer-fallowing all during the heat of mid-year, planting in the fall, and the rains had come providentially almost as soon as he was finished.

The summer-fallowing was Pa's idea. Ernie could almost hear his familiar voice saying, "This country will someday raise enough wheat to feed the nation." But to Ernie, thinking only in terms of Ma and the kids, that field meant flour and bread in plenty the coming year, cash for buying tools, clothes for the kids, maybe a little something for Ma. Too, it meant that he could hire some help in the fall for plowing.

A feeling of achievement, of pride in his own accomplishments, was all that made the continual weariness and the endless, back-breaking work bearable.

By the time he got back to the house, there was the faintest showing of gray on the horizon and a lamp burned dimly inside the sod hut. Ernie's small brother, Doug, age six months, squalled impatiently in his box-bed. Ruthie, six, was helping Ma, frying side meat and potatoes, squatting uncomfortably on the hearth. Ma, tall and worn-looking, dipped milk out of the bucket, strained it into a bottle, tied the buckskin nipple, and gave it to the baby, effectively silencing him.

She laid a hesitant hand on Ernie's shoulder, smiled just a little, murmured, "It makes a woman proud, Ernie, to have had a man like your pa—and now a boy like you."

The light increased outside until the oiled paper that covered the lone window turned gray with it. Ernie finished eating and went out, standing for a moment before the door, a ragged, unkempt figure, hair straw-colored and carelessly cut with a sharp knife. A thin tawny fuzz showed on his young-old face.

He looked southward where the sky was lightest and now he stiffened, his eyes widening with incredulity, turning smoky with smoldering anger, finally blazing with insane rage.

He screamed, "Cattle! Ma! Ma! There's cattle in our wheat!"

At his cry of alarm, Ma had snatched up the rifle, now came running with it. Ernie grabbed it from her and ran toward the cattle. Behind him she wailed, "Ernie! Don't take the gun!"

He was panting with exhaustion and helpless rage when he reached the fence, saw in a flash both how neatly it had been cut and also the tracks of horses among those of the cattle and overlying them.

"Cut fence!" he gasped. "Them cattle was drove in here!"

What he did then was governed not by reason. It was a raging, terrible fury that made him throw the gun to his shoulder, fire blindly into the bunched cattle. Then he was running, circling them through the ruined, trampled wheat, screaming childishly in his anger.

The cattle looked at him out of fear-widened, protruding eyes, lowering their horned heads and heading back for the break in the fence—all of them but one, a big, triple-wintered steer that lay struggling helplessly, his back broken by Ernie's bullet.

Quick terror flooded over the boy. He approached fearfully, saw the plain, sprawling M Spear brand on the steer's side. In a spasm of frantic fear he shouted, "Get up, damn you! Get up! Get up!"

The steer thrashed for a few long moments, then, his eyes glazing, lay still. Automatically, Ernie fished Pa's old clasp knife from his pocket and cut the animal's throat, an instinct for frugality forcing this action. With this blood on his hands, the awful consequences that would follow this unlawful deed dawned on him. He knelt beside the dead steer for a long while, shivering.

Gradually the old defiant look came back into his smarting eyes. He muttered softly, "I don't care! It warn't my fault! They got no business cuttin' fences an' puttin' them cattle in our wheat. Lordy, that's all we got. They ain't s'posed to do things like that. I don't care! I don't care!"

A plan began to hatch in his brain and he set to work feverishly. "I'll butcher this steer an' load the meat onto the wagon an' take it over to the M Spear," he whispered fiercely to himself. "Then they can't say I was stealin'. An' by golly I'll make 'em pay for the damage them critters done. I'll make 'em pay."

Struggling and fighting, sobbing softly in his fear and haste, he split the hide down the legs, skinned them, peeled the hide off one side of the animal and fought to roll it over. Sweat rolled off his forehead.

He heard the thunder of hoofs on the road, heard them muffled as the riders cut through the break in the fence and hit the softness of the wheatfield. But he did not look up. He felt trapped, like a cornered animal. He sneaked a glance at the rifle, useless without a load in it, gripped the knife until his knuckles turned white.

A glance at the steer showed him the part

of the hide that held the brand turned back in a loose flap, the brand still showing faintly through on the inside of the hide, however not so plain here as it had been on the outside, and looking strangely not like an M Spear but like an A Bar, Gus Altman's brand.

Squint Mooney thundered to a stop at the head of five others, all grinning wickedly.

"That my beef, kid?" Squint snarled viciously.

The courage of desperation came into the boys voice. "I reckon. He's mebbe worth the same as the damage you done to my wheat."

Squint laughed unpleasantly. "It ain't that easy, kid. It'll take a quitclaim on this place t' pay fer that beef. Or should I go git the sheriff? He's a cowman's sheriff, kid. He don't like them as kills the other feller's beef an' eats it."

Ernie started to protest, looked up again at the grinning faces ringing him, and stopped. "You dirty skunks!" he breathed venomously. "You rigged this an' I fell for it. Well, go on! Go on! I ain't scared!" But he was. Terribly scared.

Squint stepped from his horse. "First, I'm gonna teach you a lesson, kid. I'm gonna work you over a little so's you'll remember who owns a beef, afore you kill it."

He moved toward Ernie, lips drawn away from his teeth, hot anticipation in his slitted eyes. Ernie gripped the knife, backing, raw fear turning his face sallow, widening his eyes.

He heard Ma scream, glanced at her, saw her running toward him. Dimly in the distance, he heard Ruthie crying, heard the high-pitched wailing of the baby; closer, the pounding hoofs of a horse, the clear trill of a lark. These were things that touched him briefly and then he stiffened. *I got to take Pa's place*, he thought; *I'm the closest thing to a man Ma's got!*

Suddenly he launched himself at Squint, the knife flashing. A horse brushed against him and he felt his feet leave the ground, felt a strong hand on his collar. Then he was dangling and the horse his captor was riding fidgeted nervously, snorting. Ernie choked and turned, kicking and striking out blindly.

Gus Altman said, "Take it easy, Ernie. You're all right. You ain't fightin' this alone now." Ernie could smell the hot, lathered horse, the stink of haste and merciless spur. Gus added, "I got here just in time, but damn it, you little rooster, you got sand in your craw!"

He let Ernie down and the boy stood, knees trembling, face working, with the realization on him of what now would be happening but for Gus's arrival and help.

Gus growled, "Squint, you'll not lay a hand on that boy! An' by God you owe him for this damage an' that fence. Pay up!"

Squint let his hot glance lie on Gus's face for a moment, his hand hanging close to his gun. The men with Squint seemed to have lost interest in the proceedings. Squint, noticing this, grunted disgustedly, "You a cowman or a damned nester, Gus?"

"Never mind that. Pay up!"

Squint pointed at the steer. "How about that? How about my steer?"

Gus looked over at the half-skinned animal. His sharp eyes took in the brand on the underside of the hide, saw the plain A Bar, the other lines, not so plain, that finished the brand out into an M Spear. He gasped, surprised, angered.

"Your steer? Why you brand-changin' coyote! That's my steer! How many more you got like it?"

Squint's companions suddenly decided they had heard enough. Easing away, one of them muttered, "Gus, we didn't know about that. We didn't have no part of that!"

Ernie looked from Squint to Gus, puzzlement showing plainly on his face.

Gus was waiting, very watchful, very tense. He was expecting the move that Squint would make, the one he had to make or go to jail. This was a moment of pressure on Squint and Gus could see the effects of that growing pressure in Squint's tightened mouth, his narrowed and glittering eyes. Squint's hand flashed to the heavy Smith and Wesson .45 at his hip, thumbed back the hammer as the gun cleared the leather.

Gus yanked his Colt from his belt, shooting across his stomach. Black smoke whirled between the two. Ernie's mother screamed, fell fainting in the wheat. Squint looked over at Gus unbelievingly for an instant, then, eyes dulling, dropped heavily, a choking sound in his throat.

Silence lay across the waving wheatfield, broken only by the small sounds of the fidgeting horses and by a long, shuddering sob that escaped Ernie's white lips. Gus dismounted, resting an arm across the boy's shoulders.

"Ernie, go take your mother back to the house. I'll take care of things here. An' don't worry about the wheat. I reckon Judge Appleton'll allow you damages for that."

Tiredness fell from Ernie, replaced by a boy's hero-worshipping admiration for Gus. "Gee, thanks, Mr. Altman. I sure needed a hand when you showed up!"

Gus grinned down at him. "Reckon that's what neighbors are for, son." He turned the boy until they faced that part of the field in which wheat still grew untouched, gesturing.

"Your pa couldn't do better than that, Ernie. You're fillin' his shoes all right. Go on now. Look after your ma."

# Payday

Below him, on a small flat, Jess Holcomb could see the main herd, could see through this icy drizzle the pale glow of the fires, the hunched, slickered shapes of the other punchers.

Rain ran off his wilted hat brim, down his slickered back to the cantle of his saddle, and there soaked his seat. His hands were numb and his spirits at a low ebb, and this was shown by the bitter, discouraged lines in his young, weathered face.

Before him, he drove five cows, four of them with fat, slick calves, and three steers, his gather for the afternoon. One of the steers, a rangy, wild-eyed animal with horns half a yard long, twisting upward at varying angles, turned his huge head slowly and looked at Jess with bulging eyes, then back once again at the camp below.

Jess growled viciously, "If you break out of this bunch once more, you ornery booger, I'll bust you good!"

His words had the effect of a suggestion on the steer. Lumbering into a trot, the big animal broke out of the bunch, heading into a small patch of timber, his head high, his breath blowing in clouds of steam before him.

"All right, by God. You asked for it!" Jess set his spurs and, skidding his horse, surged into a run.

He felt the rain sting his face, felt the soggy slap of his seat against the saddle each time his horse jumped a clump of brush. He took down his rope, stiff as a board in this wet, and shook out a loop. He tore through the timber, ten feet behind the steer, dodging branches, and as the animal broke through into the open, made his throw, immediately then, setting his pony's feet in the ooze, taking his dally on the horn.

Nine hundred pounds of steer hit the end of the rope, and it snapped sharply taut. The cinch held long enough to bring the steer to his knees, and then it gave. Saddle and rider plunged off into the mud.

Jess landed on all fours, his face making the fifth contact with the mud. He was clear of the saddle and unhurt. He sat up and wiped the mud from his eyes, and his tight lips moved soundlessly, viciously, spewing vituperative words.

His saddle bobbed along fifty feet away behind the now thoroughly aroused and frightened steer. Jess glanced hastily around to see if anyone had witnessed his humiliation. His face took on a deep-red color and suddenly he leaped to his feet, jumped astride his barebacked horse, and dug his spurs cruelly, taking after the steer at a reckless, fool-hardy run, ignoring down timber and heavy brush, ignoring everything but his rage.

He had no thoughts and he made no words, but his eyes burned bright in their sockets. After a quarter-mile hard run, he came abreast of the steer, and fell off his horse reaching, grasping the long horns of the steer, his feet dragging, his muscles straining to bring the animal's huge head to earth.

"I'll take my saddle an' rope, if you don't mind," he gritted.

The steer's breath came in uneven, wheezing snorts. But his head twisted and slowly lowered, and at last, the horns on the ground, he gave up and his huge body smacked down into the mud. Jess sat on his head, a foreleg held up and back, and loosened his rope, throwing off the loop. Then he jumped off and let the steer get up. The animal glared at him for a moment, snorted once, and lumbered with ludicrous docility back toward the bunch.

Jess said grimly, "You damn fool! You beat me, an' you don't know it."

He cinched on his saddle with the end of his rope, and this way came into camp, fuming and sizzling like a stick of powder with the fuse lit. He put his little bunch with the others, and dismounted before a fire and the welcome smell of coffee.

Bob Sartor was there, hunkering close to the fire, sipping a steaming cup of coffee. He raised an eyebrow at Jess, his grin hiding behind a face overly solemn.

Jess growled, "Ain't there nothin' but this to livin'? Rain an' cold, an' heat an' dust, an' work all the time? An' at the end of the month nothin' but a bustin' headache to show for it all?"

Still too solemn, Bob said, "Guess not. But who is it under all that mud? Damned if I can recognize you, mister."

The grin started around his mouth, but then, abruptly, his expression sobered as though he had seen something in Jess's face that killed his derisive humor. He gulped the remains of his coffee, poured some more, and handed the cup to Jess.

"Have some of this. It's payday night an' you ain't one of them that has to stay with the herd. You can go to town an' wash that mud off with whiskey." He cocked an eye at Jess's saddle, cinched on with his rope. "Well, I see you got your saddle back, anyhow. You bring in the steer?"

Jess nodded with grim satisfaction. But the edge of irritation stayed with him, then and later, when they lined up at the chuck wagon, signed for the two double eagles which was their pay for the month. With this weight in his pocket, and in his mind the prospect of the warmth and gaiety of a night in town, Jess felt a little more cheerful. But this night, more than the hundreds that had gone before, the question lingered in his thoughts, *Does livin' have to be this hard?* and oddly with this fatigue and despondency in him, he could not think how good the feel of whisky in his stomach would be, but only of the headache and sickness that would follow it tomorrow. The two coins seemed pitifully little, and the thought came to him with a shock:

*They're all I've got in the world, except for a broke-down saddle an' a horse. Ten years of damn hard work an' nothin' more than this to show for it.*

He rode down the long grade into the town of Sentinel Rock with the others, and at the first crossstreet on Main, Bob Sartor pulled out of the bunch, turning right here, saying, "Drown your sorrows in redeye, boys. No headaches tomorrow for me," and his voice, while full of heavy humor, carried an overtone of eagerness that seemed very noticeable to Jess.

Now, with a whoop, the punchers spurred their horses, running down Main, scattering mud behind them in sticky, clinging gobs. Tonight, however, their enthusiasm and high spirits did not touch Jess with its contagion, and he lagged, puzzling over Bob Sartor's strange contentment as he had left them.

What Bob had was little enough, it seemed to him; indeed, not even as much as the rest of them had. Bob had a wife, true, a plain, quiet woman. They rented a two-room tarpaper shack out at the edge of town. That was where Bob's money went, and what did he have when it was all gone? He only came home two or three times a month.

Again the bitterness descended on Jess. He tied his horse and went into Satterfield's store. He bought a new pair of levis and a plaid cotton shirt, socks and underwear, and left the store with four dollars less than he had entered with. He bought a cinch at the saddle shop for a dollar and a half. He got a shave and a bath at the barbershop, changing here, and left almost another dollar for that, telling himself as he opened the door, "Four dollars for a month's smokin', an' that leaves thirty for whisky."

Out on the street, he collided with Sarah Donnell, hurrying along with her head down, slickered against the rain. "Sorry," he mumbled, and she looked up, her eyes widening, the smile immediately going across her young and pleasant face.

Now he saw who she was, and automatically he grasped her by the elbows and tossed her into the air, grinning, going through this routine that was theirs and had been since school days.

"It's muddy! You'll drop me!" she protested, but her voice held deep and unconcealed pleasure.

Jess set her down, laughing himself, his spirits miraculously lighter. "I ought to push your face in the mud like I used to," he growled, but he did not let her go, an odd reluctance in him.

She was warm and desirable, and her closeness seemed somehow to ease his ragged temper. His mind was full of a lot of things when he was close to Sarah, their childhood together, buckboard rides by moonlight, the dances down at Eph Roderick's livery barn.

But on a puncher's wages? In a tarpaper shack like Bob and Mary Sartor?

Sarah caught at his sleeve and pulled him into the doorway out of the rain. Once there, she was shy, and speechless, saying finally in a halting voice, "You ought to come see us oftener, Jess," her face was singularly still as she spoke, "How about supper tonight?"

He hesitated for a moment, said lamely, "I ought to stable my horse. I—" Her face fell before his coming refusal. He made himself grin and said, "I suppose it'd be too much to hope that there might be an apple pie? Sure, I'll come, Sarah. What time?"

"Six-thirty. And it seems to me I smelled a pie baking this afternoon. You be there in an hour."

He said, "Thanks, Sarah," watched her small form hurrying away, then turned toward the Ace-High, where horses were racked solid for a hundred feet.

He looked briefly at his own horse, head

down and hip-shot in the misting rain, thought, *Later,* and went into the smoke-filled, stuffy saloon. He got a bottle and glass at the bar, feeling this moroseness on him in his desire to be alone, and took a table against the wall.

This was the way it always started, but tonight it had to be different. For one thing, he had promised to eat at Donnells'. For another, he was so depressed that if he got drunk he'd be quarrelsome, and tomorrow would have a lot of apologizing to do to his friends. The glass sat full and untasted before him.

"You'd better drink that. You look cold enough an' sour enough that it might do you good."

Jess looked up, and forced an unwilling grin. "I was just lookin' at it an' thinkin' what a head I'd have tomorrow if I ever got started."

Lou Griggs, stocky, and swarthy, pulled out a chair, turned it and straddled it, leaning his arms on its back.

Jess stared at Lou, and his eyes took in the man's prosperous appearance, the good wool pants and vest, the gold watch chain, the fancy tooling on his gun belt and holster. Lou gambled a little, but Jess had never seen him win much. Yet he always had money.

He asked curiously, "How in hell do you do it, Lou? I never see you out breakin' your neck in the weather. If you ever need a partner you know where to look. I'm fed up."

Lou grinned, showing the gold in his heavy yellow teeth. His eyes were withdrawn and he said cautiously, "I might do that. You plumb serious?"

"You're damned right I'm serious. I'm tired of rain an' dust an' sweat. I'm tired of sittin' a saddle fourteen hours a day. I'm tired of two lousy twenties on payday."

Lou said, very softly, "I get shot at once in a while."

Something cold ran along Jess's spine, and it stopped him momentarily. Another night he would have laughed it off, gotten up and walked away, remembering the way men sometimes whispered about Lou Briggs.

But tonight he growled, "What the hell? Is that any worse than havin' a wore-out cinch break when you've got your rope on a ringy steer?"

Lou hitched his chair close, his eyes frankly measuring the depth of temper in this young puncher, and began to talk, softly, almost whispering.

"There's only one way to live without workin'. I guess you know what it is." His eyes turned hard and bored into Jess mercilessly. "You can get up an' walk away if you don't like the sound of that. But if you want to make an easy five hundred tonight, just sit still an' listen."

Jess reached for his glass and downed the fiery, amber liquid. Lou's manner angered him, and an odd recklessness made him say, "Don't be mealymouthed, Lou. Say it."

"There's a jigger in town here that's got a cool thousand salted away in a teapot. Somebody done a little careless talkin' the other day, an' I happened to hear. How'd you like half of that?"

Suspicion touched Jess, and an inner shame, which he quelled quickly. "What you want me in it for? How come you don't do it yourself, an' get it all?"

Patiently, Lou murmured, "Because this jigger is dangerous. He packs a gun an' he knows how to use it. But I figure you could get the drop on him."

"Do I know him?"

"Sure. But I ain't going to tell you who

he is. Not 'til we get there. 'Course, if you're scared—"

Perhaps it was the inner shame that made Jess say, "I'll let you know by—say eight o'clock." But he added, feeling mean and quarrelsome, "If you think I'm scared, mebbe you'd like to step outside an' find out about that?"

"Take it easy now, Jess. I didn't mean nothin'." Lou rose hastily, his eyes mirroring his inner satisfaction. "See you at eight, then," and he moved away into the crowd.

Jess poured himself another drink, downed it moodily. After several more, and feeling no better within himself, he rose unsteadily and made his way to the door, the bottle clutched by its neck in his hand. He suddenly had a desire to be away from here, as though by leaving he could shake off this feeling of uncleanliness.

"Know what I'll do," he muttered thickly. "I'll go see ole Bob. Jus' give ole Bob a drink—mebbe two-three drinks. Bet a drink'd do ole Bob good."

He thought suddenly of Sarah, and made an effort to walk straight, but the liquor on his empty stomach had done its work.

"Be all right in a minute. See Bob, then I'll go on over to Sarah's house."

Bob Sartor unsaddled in the lean-to shed back of the house, and rubbed his horse down briskly with a burlap sack, strong impatience in him, the early-lighted window of the tiny house stirring him with excitement.

When he finished, he plowed through the mud to the house, stamping vigorously on the small porch, shucking out of his soggy slicker hastily because he knew Mary would be flinging herself into his arms without regard for his wetness or the mud that was on him.

The kitchen was steamy and rich with the fragrance of cooking food. He hardly had time to drop the slicker to the floor when she was there, warm and eager and glad.

He said, "Mary," and had no time for more. There was always a newness to this experience, every time he came home.

Mary's face, grave and sweet and a little plain, changed when she looked at Bob. Somehow, what she felt for him transfigured it, and made it beautiful. It was this he saw in her, this and a hundred other things as well, that made her so dear to him.

She poured him coffee and sat him down facing her so that she could watch him as she finished preparing dinner. But he got up restlessly after a moment, reached up on the shelf, and took down a teapot with both hands—it was heavy. He took the two double eagles from his pocket, dropped one into the teapot, and laid the other on the table.

"There's enough here now for that down payment," he said. "I'll go down and see Eph Roderick in the morning and make the deal. I talked to Mr. Aldridge yesterday out at the roundup camp and he said he'd lease the place from us for winter pasture and pay five cows for the lease. If I work 'til spring, I'll be able to buy about five more. That'll be our start, Mary. By golly, we've got it now."

She paused, her hands covered with flour, and for a moment was silent, as though this thing they had worked for so long was no longer believable because it was so near. Then she breathed, "We'll be together all the time, not just once or twice a month. Bob—it'll be wonderful!"

It occurred to him suddenly that Mary was not so much interested in their having their own ranch on her account. She knew how badly he wanted it, and so she wanted it too. He nodded, smiling at her, and proud.

He thought, *There should be some kind of*

*celebration over this*, and his mind went back to the early years, and remembered what the feel of whisky was, warm and fiery in a man's stomach. He shrugged. Being with Mary, watching her, loving her, put more warmth in a man than whisky ever could.

This time of year, gray dusk lay over the land at five-thirty. Jess slipped and skidded up the cinder walk to Sartor's back door and lurched inside. He saw Bob's hand fall away from his gun, and wonder at this made him look twice at the teapot on the table. The golden content of it failed to register on him, and he waved at Bob, grinning.

"Have a drink, Bob. Have two drinks. Hell, drink the whole bottle." He ducked his head at Mary and apologized. "Sorry, ma'am. That there 'Hell' jus' slipped out."

She smiled at him, her face looking blurred, but very pretty. She brought out two glasses, and Jess poured them full, handing one to Bob, who said, "Jess, you mind if we drink to somethin'?"

"I'd like to drink to Mary, an' I'd like to drink to that teapot over there that's goin' to buy us a place of our own," Bob explained.

Sudden shock half sobered Jess. His mind working frantically, he only touched the glass to his lips. His voice was very even and quiet as he asked, "How much in that teapot, Bob?"

"A thousand. Just what it takes to get Eph Roderick's old place. We feel pretty good tonight, Jess. This is what we been savin' for so long."

Mary moved over across the room and slipped an arm about Bob's waist, looking up at him, her eyes soft and warm. Something about the two, standing together, oblivious momentarily to him—something about the warmth, the smell of food here in the kitchen, the feel of home—abruptly reminded Jess of his own home, now long gone, long forgotten. He slipped toward the door.

Bob called, "Wait a minute, Jess! You're stayin' for supper."

"Huh-uh. Thanks, but I been asked to Donnell's. Come out here a minute, Bob."

Bob came out on the stoop in the misting rain. Jess said, "A thousand in gold is a hell of a temptation to—Well, you be damned careful tonight, Bob. Somebody—Hell, be careful, will you?"

Jess's urgency must have impressed Bob, for he peered suddenly about in the darkness. "Sure, Jess. Sure I'll be careful. That money means an awful lot to Mary an' me."

Jess went down the walk, and the door closed behind him. As he rounded the house and went toward the street, he saw the blinds go down, and felt a deep relief.

*He'll be all right. Bob can take care of himself, now he's been warned. Lou Briggs ain't got the guts to tackle him alone.*

Walking toward Sarah's house, Jess felt the feeling of depression lift. It seemed long ago and unbelievable that he had considered robbery. Gold was only gold, and it wouldn't buy what he had seen in Mary's eyes as she looked at Bob. An odd feeling of having seen that look somewhere else assailed him, and suddenly he thought of Sarah and knew he had seen it in her eyes, tonight, and for years, every time she looked at him. Excitement hurried his steps.

Sarah Donnell fussed over the table, and worriedly checked each pot, steaming on the stove. "I don't see him often enough to get him interested, Mother. What can I do in an evening, two or three times a year?"

"Not much more than you're doing, honey. A woman is pretty helpless when a man won't speak."

"But he likes me. I know that. I can tell from the way he acts at the dances."

Mrs. Donnell bustled silently around the kitchen for a moment. She was trying to think back over twenty years, trying to pick out of her own experience the thing that would help Sarah. She found it, and a faint smile lightened her plump features.

"I remember your father wouldn't ask me until he had five hundred dollars in the bank. A man likes to bring something to his marriage besides his own stony-broke self."

Sarah smiled, suddenly confident. "I saw Mary Sartor today. She said Bob had enough saved with this payday to buy Eph Roderick's place. She said when she and Bob were married, *he* only had one payday in his pocket."

She grew excited. "I'll tell Jess that."

When she heard Jess's knock, she went to the door, confidence behind the quiet, sweet-lipped welcome that was on her face for him.

# The Rough String

Ted Daly, hating himself for doing it, slipped out of his seat before Miss Trent had quite finished the words, "Class dismissed," and made for the door like a cottontail scurrying to its burrow. Behind him he could hear the running feet of Clint Baggs, and the tittering of the girls. But he was faster than Clint. Unless Miss Trent called him back for rushing out this way, he had escaped Clint's large-knuckled brutal fists for one more day.

He reached the door. Still Miss Trent had not called him back, and he leaped through it with a brief, deep feeling of relief. A hasty glance over his shoulder showed him Clint, running, and Clint's gang, circling, trying to cut him off from his horse. But he had this little start, and fear lent him speed. He untied the reins with shaking fingers, mounted and laid the ends of the reins frantically on the horse's rump, hearing the jeering cries of the other boys as he galloped toward the edge of town.

With the town behind him, he could safely drop back to a walk, and this he did, now feeling the shame and regret that always washed over him. Reason told him he should make a stand, that until he did, Clint Baggs would keep him on the run, would keep this abject, crawling fear alive in him. He murmured, his face setting itself in grim lines, "Tomorrow, I got to fight him," but deep inside, he knew he would not. And there would come a day when Clint would corner him, and then . . .

Twelve on his last birthday, Ted was small for his age, and slightly built. His hair, a tawny, in-between color, neither brown nor blond, fell across his forehead in a lock that would not stay back, and stood straight out at the cowlick on the back of his head. But for all his smallness, he was active and fast, and he would have made a match for Clint, had it not been for the fear that paralyzed him.

Clint Baggs, new to the town and the school this year, had started out to whip every boy within range. He had whipped a few, and then he had started on Ted, had made him run. Promptly, then, he had forgotten the other boys and had concentrated on making life miserable for Ted.

The ride to the ranch was a matter of two hours. For the first half hour Ted's mind occupied itself with wishful thinking. To-morrow—well, maybe not tomorrow, but soon—he'd be waiting when Clint Baggs rushed out of the door. He'd be standing there, scowling, and he'd say, "You thought I was scared, didn't you? Well, I'm not." He spent a few minutes on the details of the daydream, in which he licked Clint Baggs. Then, with his cowardice vindicated by make-believe, Ted's mind turned homeward, to other things, and excitement suddenly touched him. Today Frank Jennison, his father's foreman, and the crew were to have brought home Big Black, the wild stallion, and his bunch of mares that they had suc-cessfully corraled over in the cedar breaks last week. Most of the mares were at least green-broke by now, but no one had ridden the stallion. That would be his father's job. Ted dug his heels into the aging horse, forced him into a sluggish trot.

Trotting and walking, walking and trot-ting, he came into the home ranch, sprawl-ing in a haphazard fashion over five hundred acres of sagebrush flat, and went immediately to the corral, where there was rising dust and the shrill nickering of horses and the shouting laughter of the crew.

In the act of dismounting, Ted froze, eyes widening, his face going tight with awe. There, fenced behind an eight-foot wall of stout spruce poles, pranced the wild one, Big Black. His eyes were bulging with terror, his coat was gleaming black satin. With the grace and power of a mountain lion, he would almost crouch, and then he would run at the fence that separated him from his mares, rearing against it, his sharp, small hoofs making the poles give and crack. Then he would come down, snort and rush away, only to try again.

Ted heard his father's voice through his entranced daze. "Some hoss, ain't he, Ted? Want to ride him tonight or wait 'till morning?"

The hands guffawed. Ted grinned shyly, but behind the grin was doubt and wonder. Was there an edge to their laughing? Did they know of Clint Baggs? Were they laughing because they had heard?

He decided not. Jud Gorse, the bronc buster, said loudly, "I wouldn't ride that outlaw fer a hundred dollars! Watch this." He opened the stout pole gate, and stepped in with the stallion, keeping a ready hand on the gate behind him.

Big Black didn't hesitate. Snorting, he rushed at Jud and, reaching him, reared, pawing, using his forefeet as a boxer uses his fists. Jud ducked out the gate, shooting the oak bar into place just as Big Black screamed his rage and frustration. Jud said, somewhat shakily, "See what I mean? That hoss'll kill somebody."

Frank Jennison, iron gray and shaggy as a grizzly in summer, standing close to Ted and his father, said, "Let me shoot that animal, Mr. Daly. Let me shoot him before he hurts somebody. Don't you try an' ride him."

Ted, wide-eyed, watched his father worriedly. Ross Daly, after a barely perceptible hesitation, growled, "No. Broke, he'll be the finest thing this country ever saw, and he'll get a hundred just like him. I'll try him one of these days, Frank. I've got to try him out."

Frank Jennison walked away, shaking his head, and the crew began forking hay to the mares, carrying saddles to the tack room, drifting off in voluble conversation to the bunkhouse.

Ross Daly laid a hand on Ted's shoulder

and asked, "How'd school go, Son?" more out of habit than from any curiousity, and Ted replied with the same habitual reservations, "All right." But his thoughts were saying, *How long'll it be before he hears about Clint? I got to stand up to Clint before he does.*

Away from school, he could usually imagine himself making a stand, but tonight . . . He ducked his head, broke away from his father and ran for the house. He was suddenly very ashamed in the face of his father's courage. Clint Baggs was not half so terrible as Big Black, yet his father talked of riding the outlaw, showing hardly more concern than he would when talking of riding to town in the buckboard.

As the days wore on, however, and Ross Daly kept putting off his ride, Ted began to wonder. His father seemed to have increasingly important things to do, and they kept him from the corrals where Big Black still fidgeted and fought behind the poles.

Somehow, too, Clint Baggs and the rest of the kids in school heard about the stallion and began to taunt, "When's your pa goin' to ride that horse? Mebbe he's as yella as you are, an' scared to."

And Ted, safe from Clint until school was out in the afternoon, felt a helpless rage rising in him at the bully's jibes. "My pa ain't scared of nothin'!" he would reply. "He'll ride Big Black, an' he'll break him, too! You just wait an' see!"

Evenings, Clint kept trying to corner the smaller boy, but Ted continued to elude him, saying to himself each time, "I got to fight him! I got to!"

On Thursday night, Clint tried a new tack. One of his gang pretended he had to go outside a minute or so before school let out. When Ted ran outside, he was waiting, and he made a dive at Ted, intending to hold him for Clint. If he'd made it stick, then the whole bunch would have crowded around Ted and hustled him off to the river bottom where the teacher couldn't see them. Then Clint would have had the fight he'd been spoiling for.

Ted, quick and agile, dodged the boy, and so again made good his escape. But tonight the taunts hurled at him seemed unbearable.

"Yellabelly! Your pa's a yellabelly, too! Your whole family is a bunch of yellabellies! Come on back an' fight!"

With the beginning of anger stirring in him, Ted reined his horse to a brief stop. But when the pack yelled and ran toward him, he lost heart and went on. Resenting the added cause they had for taunting him, he wondered, *Why don't pa ride Big Black? I know he ain't scared! I know he ain't!*

Ross Daly watched his son ride in, saw him pause at the corral for a look at Big Black. He had noticed his son's preoccupation of late, but had not commented on it, thinking, *If it's serious enough, he'll come to me with it.*

Now he muttered as Ted came toward him, "I've got to get time to ride that horse," and had the uneasy realization that he had been putting it off because he was afraid.

Ted paused before him embarrassedly, turning red. He stammered something unintelligble, then blurted, "Pa, why don't you ride him? You scared of him?"

On the point of denying this, Ross Daly observed the intent concentration in the boy's face and realized in time, *It's not an idle question he's asking. For some reason it's important to him.*

He answered softly, "I guess I am, Ted. I guess that's why I've been putting it off."

Disbelief came first to Ted's face. Then it seemed to sag into lines of complete despair. Ross Daly felt obligated to explain, "Fear is nothin' to be ashamed of, boy. All of us have it. Nature provides fear so that animals, human and otherwise, will stay alive. Big Black is scared to death. If I opened the corral gate, his first instinct would be to escape. That would be fear working. But then he'd likely think of his mares. That's his responsibility. He'd overcome his fear thinking of it, and he'd probably stay long enough to tear down a few fences an' take the mares with him. I reckon I'll ride Big Black tomorrow. I guess I haven't been facin' facts. Once a man gets to avoidin' things, because he's afraid of them, then it's time for him to do somethin' about it."

He saw relief in Ted's face, and something that looked like determination. The boy grinned uncertainly at him, and Ross Daly thought, *I'll get up at daylight. By the time he heads out for school, I'll have that job done.*

Ted heard his father get up as gray seeped over the horizon, staining the night sky with its drabness. Hastily he crammed himself into his clothes, tiptoed to the door and slipped into the chill air. Down at the corral, he heard Big Black's nervous snorting, the pounding of his hoofs as he thundered around the tiny corral. He heard his father's soothing talk, and he ran, muttering softly, "Don't get on him 'till I get there, Pa."

As he came around the corral fence and crouched there, a rope snaked out and settled over Big Black's head. Screaming shrilly, the stallion charged the man, and Ross Daly scrambled over the fence, landing ten feet from Ted, not seeing him. He dallied the rope there and, circling the corral, climbed over and again dropped inside. Again, Ted heard a rope whisper as it was thrown, and again the stallion screamed and charged.

But this time, the first rope had brought him up short, and at that instant Ross Daly dallied the other rope, murmuring between his teeth, "All right. Now you know the feel of a rope. Let's see if you like a saddle as well."

Opening the gate, he carried his saddle inside. New fury seemed to inject itself into the stallion. Rearing and pawing, he fought with but one purpose, to break loose and destroy this man. The corral poles creaked and popped from the strain. Ted murmured, suddenly realizing that he was bathed in sweat, "Don't do it, Pa! Don't do it! He'll kill you!" He had the urge to run, screaming, to rouse the crew, but he set his teeth and controlled it.

The ropes, tight about the stallion's neck, were shutting off his wind, and now his breathing came harshly from flaring nostrils. But he gave one last surge at this hated man, putting all his strength in it, and with a report like that of a pistol, the rope snapped. Ross Daly heard it and dropped his saddle, kicking up dirt with his feet as he frantically lunged into a run.

Ted saw his father would not make it, saw him dive to the ground, rolling. Vicious hoofs came down where he had fallen, and for a moment Ted thought the stallion had caught him. But Ross Daly was up, running again, and this time he made it over the fence, a hair's breadth ahead of the maddened horse.

Ted heard his breathless, hoarse whisper, "To blazes with you! I'll have Frank shoot you. Why should I get my neck broke to prove to myself I ain't afraid of you? I am scared of you, an' you know it, don't you?"

Ted thought suddenly, *He don't know I'm here, but if he did* . . . Without thinking further, he ran softly and silently to the house. He went up on the porch, opened the door, slammed it without going in. Then, whistling, he made his way again toward the corral. Arriving there, he asked, forcing concerned eagerness into his breathless voice, "You ain't rode him, yet, have you Pa? I wanted to see you do it. I got up early so's I could."

"No, and I ain't gonna. . . ." Ross paused. "No, I ain't rode him yet, boy, but I will! Right now!"

Tension started building up in Ted as his father came back from the tack room with a couple of new ropes. What if his father was hurt, maybe even killed? Fear was a part of the instinct of self-preservation, Pa had said. Maybe you shouldn't ignore it this way. He had the urge to call out, "Don't do it, Pa!" But he kept his lips still.

Ross Daly put another rope on Big Black and dallied it tight. He put a rope on Big Black's forefoot, then, holding that rope in one hand, his saddle in the other, he approached cautiously. Big Black reared. As he came down, fidgeting for balance, Ross lunged back, taking a strain on the forefoot and spilling the horse neatly. Four times he spilled the stallion on the ground, and after the fourth upset the horse stood trembling, breathing hard as Ross Daly approached, moving as far from the man as the ropes would allow.

Ross Daly laid a hand on the stallion's neck. He snorted and lunged against the ropes. His breathing was labored and came in shrill whistles. Ross Daly touched his neck again. On went the hackamore and the horse whirled and lashed out with his heels. Ross Daly jumped clear and spilled Big Black again with the rope on his forefoot. As the animal rose, on went the blanket and saddle.

Ted looked at his father's face. It was streaming sweat and was a ghastly gray. Big Black threw off the saddle and whirled, kicking it halfway across the corral. Ross Daly recovered it, carried it back. Again he spilled Big Black, and this time he got the saddle cinched.

Ted muttered, seeing the way Big Black's eyes rolled at his father, the way he tried to keep away, "You've got him scared of you now, Pa." And, "Oh, I wish this was over!"

Now Ross Daly got a gunnysack from the corral fence and flung it over Big Black's head in one motion that shut off the stallion's sight. He tied it down while the animal's muscles twitched and jumped. He said, hoarsely, his own breath coming in gasps,

"He's ready to ride now. Wait till I get the ropes off!"

He went across the corral and loosened his dally there, then went back and flung off both ropes. The horse fidgeted and snorted weakly, but his feet were anchored to that one spot by his blindness.

Now Ross Daly shook loose the loop on the stallion's forefoot, and, with one smooth motion, he was in the saddle, his feet firmly anchored in the stirrups.

Ted thought he had seen a fight already. But as the blindfold came off, he changed his mind. For one instant, the horse stood motionless, then he exploded.

Ted screamed, "Look out!" as the stallion reared, lost his balance from the unaccustomed weight on his back and fell forward with a crash. But Ross Daly had ridden wild ones before, though never one so rough as this. He was out of the saddle, leaping aside, and when Big Black scrambled to his feet, Ross Daly was again sitting the saddle.

Now the horse bucked around and around, crashing against the poles in an attempt to crush his rider's leg. But each time he hit, Ross Daly jerked his leg free, raising it, and when Big Black would sheer away, down it would go again.

Ted thought the struggle would never stop. His father was unashamedly hanging onto the saddlehorn. Blood streamed out of his nostrils, bright red against the pallor of his face. But now, as the horse slowed, he raked him with his spurs, from neck to flank.

The crew streamed out of the bunkhouse, ludicrous in their bright red flannels, pulling on jeans, rubbing sleep out of their eyes, yelling, "Ride 'im, boss! Yah-hoo! Ride him!"

Big Black was slowing. Even the spurs failed to urge him into renewed effort. He stopped, finally, his head hanging dejectedly. Ross Daly yelled, triumph killing his utter fatigue. "Open the gate! Open the gate an' I'll give him a ride!"

Ted jumped to the gate and swung it open. Spurring again, Ross rode the stallion out and galloped off into the dawn.

Jud Gorse yelled, "By golly, I told you jiggers the boss wasn't scared of him! I told you he'd ride 'im."

Frank Jennison shook his shaggy head slowly, his face solemn. He murmured to Ted, "Your dad's a real one, boy, He was scared, half scared to death, but he rode him anyway. You been here watchin' all the time?"

Ted nodded. The crew trooped back to the bunkhouse, but he waited. His mind was busy, and suddenly he thought of Clint Baggs.

Today he'd fight Clint. Today he just had to fight Clint. But with the memory in him of how his own presence had stiffened his father's courage, he said to his father as the latter rode up, worn out, but grinning. "You s'pose you could come to town this afternoon an' pick me up?"

Ross Daly stared uncomprehendingly for a moment, but something he saw in Ted's sober face checked his hasty refusal. Instead, he replied, "Mebbe. Why?"

"I want to show you somethin'. You tie the buckboard down in that clump of willows in the river bottom behind the school an' watch. You just watch without lettin' anybody see you. Will you?"

Ross Daly nodded and slid down off Big Black, who was now docile with exhaustion.

Nervousness began to build in Ted, just thinking of this afternoon. He believed he'd have the courage to fight Clint. But it didn't hurt a man to have someone watching to stiffen his back when it needed stiffening the most.

As he went toward the house with his father the thought occurred to him, *I don't have to run anymore.*

A weight he had been carrying for a long time seemed to have vanished abruptly. He grinned up at his pop, and the two went into the kitchen together, drawn by the odor of bacon and flapjacks and coffee.

# The Winter of His Life

In afternoon, the porch was shaded by the shabby red-brick wall of the house. The old man sat in the padded rocker, his gentle motion making a steady and unchanging squeak. Sun heat beat against the pavement beyond the small square of lawn, to rise in shimmering layers that had the effect of distorting shapes across the street. A red and white jeep tinnily announced its presence to the tune of "Yankee Doodle," and the shabby, overcrowded houses along River Street erupted unbelievable numbers of small, dirty children, who ran to the curb, nickels clutched in grimy hands, to wait for the man with the ice-cream sticks.

A truck made its throaty racket, passing the ice-cream wagon, and from long habit the old man held his breath for the children's safety. When the truck had passed, he resumed his rocking.

Inside the house he could hear the busy whir of Mary's sewing machine. He thought of Mary, his mind seeing her black-haired and young, with a devil of merriment dancing in her eyes. She was not like that anymore. She was aged and weathered, as he himself was.

Time made changes, in people as in trees and houses and cities. Those two great cottonwoods that shaded the yard had been but saplings when the old man came here. The street in front had been dusty. Quite a nice new neighborhood, it had been. Respectable.

Now there was the slaughterhouse down next to the river, reddening the stream for a half-mile below it. There were warehouses, a trucking company's dock, a beer joint on either corner. There were the familiar sounds of violence at night, the wail of the police sirens.

A car prowled along the river, hesitated before the old man's house, and finally stopped. A youngish man got out and sauntered up the walk, casually and unhurriedly opening the wrought-iron gate.

His tone was deferential. "Mr. Handy? Pete Handy?"

"Yep." This was an old story to old Pete Handy. Another newspaperman—maybe a writer of fiction. Poking around in the rubble of the past he had become interested in Pete Handy, perhaps in some happening to which Pete Handy had been a witness. He wanted Pete Handy to talk.

But there was no stimulation in recalling the past now. It was too long dead, too long buried. He had hashed and rehashed too many times the things he had done, the things he had seen, until at last they assumed in his mind the unreality of lurid fiction.

This one would be no different from the others. He would ask Pete about something and, when Pete answered, would disagree, would politely argue, for some of the things he had read would not jibe with what Pete told him. Pete might say, as he had often said before, "Man, I was there," and that would draw the courteous but skeptical, "Yes, sir. I know you were. But perhaps you've forgotten. North's *Old Time Gunmen* says. . . ."

The conversation took the pattern he had known it would take. He made his answers to the questions wearily, giving this only a part of his mind. The noise of the city went on, trucks, distant locomotives, the roar of a motor back in the alley and the squeal of tires against hot pavement, the interminable whir of Mary's sewing machine, the drone of a fly.

The young man went away, wearing an expression that was both puzzled and pitying, and the old man rocked away the afternoon, tall and gaunt, his skin like cracked, old leather stretched tightly over a bony frame. His eyes were faded blue, his hands blue-veined and frail on the rocker's arms. Only his mind was active.

Abilene, Dodge City, Deadwood, Tombstone. The trouble centers of the early West. Wyatt Earp, Bat Masterson, Hickok, Billy the Kid. Lincoln County War, Johnson County War. The sight of a million ponderous buffalo in one herd. Ninety-six, the old man was, and these were the things he had seen.

He had felt the kick of a Colt's single action against his palm, had seen a man fall before him—more than once. He carried bullet scars, and knife scars, and the scars of a longhorn's hooves.

His name had inspired respect, and sometimes fear. But that was past. Oddly, it was not the people he recalled now, nor the conflict. It was the everlasting peace of a thousand miles of unfenced, unpeopled land. It was the brassy blue of the sky on a hot day, the yellow rippling movement of an infinity of virgin grass. It was the freedom a man could know. . . .

A bunch of boys, teen-agers, moved past on the walk, their faces molded into the conscious pattern of toughness, their words secret and softly spoken. The old man watched them and drew their hostile stares. One of them, Joe Nemecek, he knew, for he had ridden him on his old and bony knee as a baby so many years ago. He knew Frank Sanchez, too. The others were familiar but unknown strangers, come to the community during these last ten years, the years of final deterioration. Joe Nemecek was a stranger too, impatient of age, busy with his own dark pursuits, forgetful of a childhood friendship.

Pete Handy could see the pattern of viciousness in the group, the immature, childish savagery so dangerous when the body is grown, when the mind still retains the cruelty of childhood and has not yet learned to pity.

He shrugged, and the boys passed from his sight. These things were no longer the old man's problems. There had been a time when he would have carefully catalogued each boy as a potential source of danger to himself. But that, too, was long ago, when he had been a peace officer himself.

The sewing machine stopped its whirring. In the depths of the house, in the kitchen, he heard the metallic clang of a skillet being withdrawn from a cupboard. Afterward he heard the sizzle of frying meat and smelled its sharp and friendly odor.

The shadows lengthened along the street. Brief, home-going traffic clogged the artery that was River Street, and then the quiet of dusk came down.

Frank Sanchez said: "See that old buzzard? I was in the store this morning when he came in after a loaf of bread. He carries his change in a black pocketbook, but he didn't have no change this morning. He pulled out a roll of bills two inches thick, tied with a rubber band."

Joe Nemecek broke in. "He goes for a walk every night at eight. Down to the slaughterhouse for a word with the night watchman. He skirts the truck dock and goes to the riverbank, where he stands and has a smoke. Then he goes home."

A third broke in with hopeful wickedness, "Tonight?"

"All right."

Joe Nemecek felt a stir of excitement, but he felt none of the fear which the prospect of the first attack had stirred in him some months before. They were so easy—so damned easy. They crawled and they begged and they whimpered. You got so you could feel nothing but contempt for them. It got so it was like stepping on a beetle, and you felt nothing afterward. Yet, in prospect, there was always this excitement, this tingling anticipation.

Some of them died, some recovered. You left them in the shadows limp and inert and bloody, and what happened after that didn't matter.

The planning was brief. "Down behind the slaughterhouse at eight," said Sanchez. "We'll spot him as he goes around the truck dock and slip ahead of him to the riverbank."

They broke up at the corner. Sanchez and a couple of others went into the beer joint. Joe Nemecek went home.

Joe's home was one of the old ones, new at the same time the old man's house had been new. Joe's father, stolid and round-backed from a long lifetime of hard work, was puttering in the neat, postage-stamp plot of grass before the house.

There was too much age-difference between Joe and his father for there to be any closeness. Joe was seventeen; his father, sixty. Joe said, "Hi," and drew his father's habitually unfriendly stare. Jan Nemecek had no patience with the indolence and wastrel prowling of his son.

Nor did the boy feel patience for his father's stolidity, his unimaginative beast-of-burden attitude toward his work. Mainly the gulf between them was there because of Jan Nemecek's patient acceptance which he had learned in his hard sixty years—because of the restless reaching for something better which stirred in the boy.

"You better get them fool notions outa your head," Jan would say, "Livin' is work—an' work—an' more damn work. Stay away from them bums you run with. Git yourself a job."

And be like you? Joe would think. Be a damned workhorse like Sol Levy's junk horse an' stand with your head down while they lay on the whip? Starve and work and worry until you don't know anything else? Not me!

Resentment was the seed of his discontent, resentment against monotony that could dull your mind, rob you of courage, make you grovel and beg like the ones Joe remembered, bleeding and dying in the ugly shadows.

He tramped up the flagstone walk, across the sagging porch that needed paint, and into the musty house, a tall boy, stringy from sudden, upshooting growth, wearing dirty levis and a white T-shirt.

At eight o'clock, the old man laid aside his paper and got up. His wife looked at him over the sock she was darning in her grave and unsmiling way, and weariness showed in her eyes, weariness that never left her these days. "You shouldn't walk alone in the dark. This is not the same neighborhood that it was when we came here. There's a bad gang of boys. . . ."

"Joe Nemecek? I used to ride him on my knee, and often enough found it wet afterward. Frank Sanchez? I taught him how to catch a baseball. The others? They're not bad, Mary. They're only young."

The things that youth felt and dreamed did not change with the years. The heady wine of adventure stirred forever in their growing and active bodies. They needed something to pit themselves against, and in the old days these things had been plentiful.

Then it had been adventure just to stay alive. There had been the long cattle drives, monotonous and back-breaking to be sure, but filled with danger and excitement. Living had been a battle against the elements. Running cattle had been a battle against those who would enrich themselves at your expense. Youth needed something to fight.

Pete Handy could remember Dodge, filled to overflowing with trail hands no older than Joe Nemecek, wanting perhaps the same things Joe Nemecek wanted: a drink, a fight, a spin of the wheel. Excitement.

There was little enough of that to be had any more. The country was tamed. You conformed to the pattern or you ran afoul of the law. Yet civilization could not still the eternal longings of youth. . . .

The night was cool, and the old man took a light sweater from its hook in the hall closet. His hand touched something hard and smooth, groped, and drew out the worn leather cartridge belt and holstered .45. The tools of his trade. He fingered them for a moment, then hung them back in the closet. They had an unfamiliar feel in his hands, an unfamiliar and slightly unpleasant feel.

He went into the cool darkness, hardly

hearing the clang of the iron gate behind him.

Slowly he walked, his mind fallow and inactive. The slaughterhouse was a dim and untidy shape of clustered buildings against the aurora cast in the sky by the city's lights. The truck dock was brightly lighted, busy and noisy. Great, long trailers stood backed against it, side by side. On both corners the beer joints put the red neon glow of their signs on walk and pavement. The river lifted its cool, dark smell.

At the slaughterhouse, a dark shape waited behind the chain link gate, shadowy and still. The light pleasant odor of pipe tobacco smoke came to Pete Handy and he said: "Hello, Ben. How does it go tonight?"

"All right. Quiet."

Pete Handy packed his pipe and lighted it. They smoked in silence for a while, companionable silence. The breeze shifted, bringing the smell of the slaughterhouse, and even this had the power to stir Pete Handy's memory. The smell of death. The smell of ten thousand naked and blackened buffalo carcasses rotting slowly on the plain. The smell that hung over the land the spring after the big die-up.

He murmured something to Ben and

moved away, stiff and old in the winter of his life. He skirted the truck dock at the circle of its light and took the narrow path through the brush to the river's bank.

Out of his past came the old tingle of premonition, the sixth sense that had half a dozen times saved his life. It was uneasiness, it was a stirring in the follicles of the hair that grew on the back of his neck. An animal sense, one he had not felt for fifty years.

This time he reasoned it away. The smell of the slaughterhouse with its attendant memories had caused it. It was nothing. This was the city.

Sudden movement came from the shadows. Against the light on the water's surface was dimly silhouetted the shape of a man—no, not a man, but one of those mixtures of man and boy. Man's body, boy's mind. Man's strength, boy's cruelty.

A voice, clear and soft said: "All right. Get him!"

They came in from all sides, uncounted by the old man, who stepped back, whose hand went automatically from some ancient prompting to his side where no gun hung tonight.

A fist slammed against his jaw, snapped

his head to one side. He was slow with age, but all of the old, remembered things came back. Groggy, he still went through the motions, and while there was no hope in him, neither was there fear, or even regret.

Waiting in the high willows beside the whispering river, Frank Sanchez asked: "Who the hell is he anyway? Where's he get his money? Old-age pension?"

The tension was upon Joe Nemecek, the tension that always preceded these things. "What difference does it make? He used to be some kind of a cop. Maybe he's got a cop's pension." Cop or not, he would die, cringing and begging against the hard-eyed lack of pity that surrounded him. His body would go into the river and would catch on the rocks beneath the viaduct three hundred yards below.

Movement stirred along the path, and the old man came out of the willows. Frank Sanchez said: "All right. Get him!"

Frank moved close, and his fist slammed against the side of the old man's jaw. Joe Nemecek came in, wanting part of this, and was briefly surprised at the way the old man stood, spraddle-legged, a little crouched. A couple of the gang moved behind him to close the path, to cut off retreat; but there was no retreat in the old man.

Even as this flurry of action moved toward its inevitable climax, Joe Nemecek could feel surprise at this, for it was something new. There was only silence from the old man, and harsh bellows of his breath dragging in and out. Frank Sanchez moved his body too close, and the old man's knee came savagely into Frank's crotch and put him down on the ground, rolling and groaning.

They beat the old man inexorably backward. Joe came close, his hands fisted and ready to strike. Suddenly it was very important to him that he make the old man break, that he make him beg and crawl as the others had done.

The dull shine of the river put its glow on the old man's face, put its pinpoint of sparkle in the fierce old eyes—uncompromising, bitter, yet showing some strange and savage pleasure. Fear had not touched him, and suddenly Joe Nemecek knew that fear would never touch him.

Joe dropped his hands and yelled: "Stop it! Cut it out!"

Frank Sanchez, rising, snarled, "What the hell?" and came in, fisting a rock the size of an orange in his hand. The rock came against the side of the old man's head with a sudden crack and Pete Handy tottered and fell, limp on the wet sand. Frank straddled him immediately, drawing back the fisted rock.

The brutality of it infected them all, lusting and bright-eyed, all save Joe Nemecek. He caught the upraised hand of Sanchez and twisted the rock away. He brought it around against Frank's head, and felt the slump of the older boy. He flung Sanchez aside, then stood himself straddling the old man, but facing the gang.

He did not know what to say: he could not even fathom his own foolishness. "He wasn't afraid," he said. "He didn't even beg. Let him alone."

It was a tight and touchy moment, but Joe Nemecek found an intoxicating excitement in it. This was something new for Joe.

The way the old man stood, unyielding, turned them back, turned them unsure and boyish again and sent them slinking away. Joe knelt over the limp and lifeless body of the old man, feeling pity for the first time in his life.

A siren wailed distantly. Frank Sanchez rose, cursed him, and went away. The siren wailed again. Joe looked at the old man. Joe hated cops, and this one had been a cop. Yet, for an instant, he could not help wondering how the years had been with this one, what he had done and what he had seen, what he had learned that had made him able to die so courageously. For an instant he imagined himself, Joe Nemecek, blue-clad, behind the wheel of that distant police car, no workhorse, but a man with a job to do.

He rose and walked toward home, frowning.

The old man lay by the riverbank and stared sightlessly at the sky. He had found again the everlasting peace of a thousand miles of unfenced, unpeopled land.

# They Called Him a Killer

## Chapter I
## The Angry Kid

Sundown was a relief after the blistering day. With but a couple of miles yet to go, Stuart Cannon dismounted at a narrow stream and flung himself flat on the ground to drink from its tepid, alkali water.

The flat stones of the creek bed were hot, as though a fire burned beneath them, and Cannon got up quickly with a surprised, low-voiced curse. He rubbed the scorched palms of his hands against the legs of his dusty pants.

Downstream, the horse sucked noisily, greedily, his hide caked with sweat and dust. In the west, the sun turned the sky to copper.

For a moment, Cannon was still, relaxed and motionless. Then he turned, unbuckled his saddle cinch and lifted the saddle off to cool the horse's sweaty back. The horse shook himself.

An almost negligible breeze stirred and Cannon faced into it gratefully, fishing without thought in his stained, damp shirt pocket for sack tobacco and papers. He squatted comfortably while he rolled his smoke and touched a match to its end.

A youngish man in his early twenties, he was neither tall or overly broad. Slight, you would say, until you noticed the breadth of his shoulders and the ripple of muscles under his tight shirt.

His face bore several small hairline cuts, for he had dry-shaved this morning in anticipation of his arrival. It was smooth-skinned, a dark-bronzed face whose careful lack of expression made it notable. The eyes were dark, almost black. The brows were also dark, unusually bushy, and made an almost unbroken line across the bridge of his nose, which was straight and somewhat narrow.

This was the face of a man alone, neither accepted by nor accepting society—a man who knew conflict, and struggle, and rejection, and who had withdrawn into himself as a defense.

There was an oddly brooding look to his face, a dark wariness about his eyes. His cheeks were hollow, his cheekbones high. Strong-jawed, firm-lipped, you could imagine neither laughter nor softness ever changing the rigid mold of countenance. Strangely enough, it was this very quality about him which most attracted women. Perhaps his coldness simply presented a challenge. Or perhaps they sensed the warmth so carefully guarded beneath it.

In dress, he conformed to a conventional pattern—down-at-the-heel boots, cracked with age and use; dusty, faded waist overalls; blue shirt, now darkened at armpits, back and chest with sweat; and narrow-brimmed hat, its crown round and uncreased.

An aged gun rode low at his right side in an age-hardened holster, but the loops in his cartridge belt were empty of cartridges.

Things pegged a man. Those empty loops pegged Stuart Cannon as a man who carried a gun more from habit and compliance with custom than from any real need. They shouted plainly that he expected the loads in the gun itself to be sufficient for any trouble he was likely to encounter.

Hard, he looked—hard and possessed of a vast competence. So strongly, in fact, did he emanate confidence that the gun seemed unnecessary. You'd look at him twice, wherever you saw him. But he would not draw you with liking as some men do. Rather, he would stir in you the vaguest kind of uneasiness.

If you analyzed it, as few ever did, you would be reminded of a cat, tolerating human society only because tolerance served its purpose, but never really liking it.

This was Stuart Cannon, and he was only what circumstances had made him.

Now, he turned his head and stared in the direction he had been traveling, his face sour with distaste.

There it stood, its bleak-gray walls rising like an obscene monument out of the desert floor. Gray walls, topped with steel spikes and broken glass. Gray walls, whose tiny windows were barred with steel.

Anger flared briefly in Cannon's eyes, and impatience as well. But he waited until he had finished the cigarette before he stirred. Then he rose and flung the stinking, soggy saddle blanket onto the horse's back. He followed it with the saddle, which he cinched rather loosely. Then he swung himself up and moved out again in the direction of the prison.

There would be, he knew, a town at the

prison's base, a town with narrow, littered streets which were more like alleys than anything else. The houses would be squat, flat-roofed adobes, housing an abundance of dirty, dark-skinned children. There would be the inevitable strings of bright peppers hanging from projecting beams, and at this time of day the still air would be filled with the sharp aroma of spicy cooking and cedar woodsmoke.

Dogs would pick Cannon up by his strange smell at the edge of town and would follow him, yapping savagely, wherever he went.

The largest building in town would probably be the Mission of San Marcos. No doubt it would stand facing the Plaza, or village square.

And after his interview with Fr. Gonzales, Stuart Cannon would find a cantina where he'd eat supper of food that burned him from the tip of his tongue clear to the bottom of his stomach.

He liked none of it, this baked, blistering country, its food, its people, the errand which brought him here.

Then why had he come? Even now, Cannon did not thoroughly understand the why himself. It began, he thought, with a man escaping from prison. No. It began a lot further back than that. Perhaps, in reality, the escape was the end—or the beginning of the end.

Still frowning at his own thoughts, Cannon reached the outskirts of the town, which differed in no respect from what he had expected. Three skinny, mangy dogs picked him up and followed, yapping and snapping at his horse's heels. Cannon cursed them silently in his mind.

All roads led to the Plaza, and Cannon reached it as gray dusk filtered down through the hot, still air to settle on it.

He cut across the treeless, dusty square, threading its way between two ancient brass cannon, now green-black with corrosion. The dogs quit him on the far side in favor of another dog which they appoached in their stiff-legged way, hair bristling, teeth bared. The other dog quivered and his tail whipped between his legs, and then the three were on him, snarling and biting until he gained his feet and fled with the three in full cry after him.

Watching, Cannon's face showed a certain cynical bitterness, for he had seen this pattern often repeated in human society.

An idler plucked a plaintive melody from

the strings of a guitar, seeming not to notice Cannon but studying him closely all the same. Somewhere, in the distance, a woman screamed imprecations at a silent faceless husband. A child squawled, closer, and somewhere, a jackass brayed.

Cannon dismounted before the mission, a large, adobe building with the usual twin square towers topped with bell cupolas. Between the towers, a cross silhouetted itself against the darkening sky.

With his eyes rather bleak, Cannon took time to roll another cigarette and smoke it thoughtfully. His eyes touched the idler, paused and passed on. Finally he tossed the cigarette away, frowned and went up the walk toward the mission door.

He removed his hat and ran a hand through his sweat-plastered hair, showing the first uncertainty apparent in him today. Then, with obvious irritation at this, he pushed open the door and went inside.

It was cool here, cool because of the three-foot-thick adobe walls, because of the high, vaulted ceiling. Down at the altar, a black-robed woman was kneeling, praying. Cannon stared at her briefly before his eyes began their nervous wandering.

It was, he realized, the first time he had

been in a church since boyhood . . . since
. . . His expression hardened.

Damn it, that was over. It had been hard
to forget, hard to stop hating so bitterly.
But he'd managed it. And now it was all
going to be dug up again, a dead thing, long
buried, its ugliness exposed to the light of
day.

Candles flickered from the altar, furnish-
ing the only light until a black-robed priest
came in carrying a lighted taper. The priest
saw him, changed direction and approached.
The priest murmured, *"Espere un momento,
señor,"* caught himself and said softly in En-
glish, "A moment, my son." He continued
then, lighting other candles in their wall
brackets and returning at last to the uncom-
fortable Stuart Cannon.

Cannon's voice was flat, sounding unnat-
urally loud and clear, "I'd like to see Father
Gonzales."

The priest smiled. "I am Father Gonzales.
And you are Stuart Cannon. Am I correct?"

Cannon nodded. He supposed there was
some resemblance between himself and his
father, which would account for the priest's
recognition.

Father Gonzales was a small, graying,

160

gentle man a head shorter than Cannon. His face, dark as antique leather, was seamed with deep creases, giving him an almost gnomish look. He led the way through a door and into a small, austerely finished room with bare walls of naked adobe.

It was the coolest place Cannon had been all day. Under the influence of the cool, and of the priest's quiet manner, Cannon felt some of his irritability fading.

The priest said, "You look tired. Some wine, perhaps?"

"Water would be better—if it's cool."

From a tall olla jar, the priest took a dipperful of water. The jar was made of some kind of porous clay which allowed the contents to seep through and evaporate on the outside. Cannon was pleasantly surprised at the water's coolness. He handed the dipper back, refusing a second drink with a spare shake of his head, and came quickly to the point, "Your letter said that he'd escaped. Have they caught him yet?"

Father Gonzales shook his head. His glance was searching, probing, as though Cannon were a printed page which he wished to read and understand. Cannon's next question was a trifle irritable. "Well, what do you want of me? The law can handle this well enough. The law can catch him and bring him back. Why did you have to bring me into it?"

The priest smiled, "Why did you come into in, my son?"

Anger stirred in Cannon's eyes. "Why? Because you asked me to, that's why. I ought to have had better sense."

"That is not what I meant. I meant to ask why you came. You could have refused. You could have closed your mind to your father's trouble and I would not have blamed you if you had."

Cannon had been wondering the same thing himself for the past five or six days. He said honestly, "I'm not sure. Maybe I came because he's the last blood relation I've got. I've got no use for him, but . . ."

It was obvious that Cannon liked his thoughts to be straight and uncomplicated. Self-doubt was foreign to him and he didn't like it. He growled, "Exactly what do you want from me? You think I can catch him when the law can't?"

The priest's face showed considerable understanding. He murmured, "It was not catching him that I had in mind. It is inevitable that your father will be caught—or

162

killed. It was only to prevent his being killed that I sent for you."

Cannon asked rather brutally, "Why should I care whether he's killed or not? You're forgetting what he did to me, what he did to my mother. It took me a long time to stop hating him. Now you want to stir it all up again."

The priest's tone had a forced quietness, "Yet you do care—else you would not have come. You are, after all, his son."

Cannon laughed harshly, "Don't hold that against me. I had nothin' to do with it."

His anger was rising, anger directed more at himself than at the gentle priest. He said, "Your concern for his life is misplaced. He should have been hung years ago. He's an escaped murderer. He killed my mother in a drunken rage and worst of all he didn't even remember doing it."

"That is what the jury decided."

## Chapter II
## Flesh and Blood

Cannon didn't even seem to hear. His eyes were brooding, blank. Softly, almost as though he were thinking aloud, he said, "I was twelve when it happened. I had a home, a mother, a father. I went to school and I was just like anybody else. Then one morning I woke up and I had nothing. My mother was dead. My father was in jail for killing her."

He shuddered involuntarily with the vividness of this memory. "I came into the kitchen just like I always did. The sun was shining in through the curtains. I heard people talking and I came into the kitchen and saw her lying on the kitchen floor. Nobody'd moved her or covered her. There was blood all over her. Her hair was matted with it. It was splattered all over the floor. Beside her was a whisky bottle that had been used to beat her to death."

Cannon's face was pale. "They said they found my father passed out not far from where she lay."

He looked at the priest dazedly. "Hate's a thin word for what I felt toward him. Hate kept me going for a good many years afterward. It was all I had.

"After the funeral, nobody seemed to know what to do with me. They said I'd turn out just like him and no one wanted to take me in. But you can't leave a twelve-year-old to shift for himself, can you? So they talked the stableman into taking me. He wanted a free hired hand in the stable anyway. He took me out of school and I curried horses and forked hay and cleaned stalls from daylight to dark seven days a week. If he'd catch me sleeping, he'd wake me up with a strap. So I ran away.

"There's more, but it all sounds the same. When I was eighteen I only weighed a hundred and ten pounds. I'd been kicked out of more towns and boarded in more jails . . ." He snorted disgustedly. "Not because of anything I did, either. But because I was broke, and dirty, and hungry."

He stopped, breathing hard, mildly surprised at the way he had uncorked the years of bitterness.

The priest's voice was soft. "That's all past."

"Sure, I know it's past. I stopped hating him a long time ago. But don't tell me I owe him anything just because I happen to be his son."

The priest sighed. He said patiently, "Do you know where your father has gone?"

Impatiently, Cannon said, "How should I know where he's gone?"

"He has gone back to Red Butte."

The significance of that failed to register

on Cannon's consciousness. He said, "If you know where he's gone it ought to be simple enough to catch him. Was he fool enough to tell you where he was going?"

Father Gonzales shook his head. "He said nothing. But I know. Does it mean nothing to you that he should go to Red Butte?"

"It means he was a damn fool," Cannon growled.

Father Gonzales ignored the profanity. "No. It means that he knew he had not killed your mother. It means that he returned to Red Butte to try to find out who did."

Cannon mocked with impatient disgust, "Now I've heard everything. He spends more than ten years in prison not knowing what happened that night because he was too drunk to know. And then suddenly he decides he's innocent. What gave him that idea?"

The priest looked somewhat abashed. "Perhaps I had something to do with it." He went on hurriedly before Cannon could interrupt. "I grew to know your father very well during the years he was here. He confided in me. I learned, among other things, that your father and mother very rarely

166

quarreled. If that were true, there would have been no motive for his killing her, for only during a violent quarrel could he have done what they say he did."

Cannon shook his head. "It won't jell, and you know it won't. My mother had no enemies. She was universally liked and respected in Red Butte. She helped them have their babies and nursed them when they were sick. She belonged to the church. You can cross out robbery as a motive because we were poor and everyone knew it. And women aren't murdered without a mighty powerful reason."

"That is true. But I'm not convinced. I've been at this prison for many years, my son. I have known thousands of convicts during that time—the weak—the vicious—the bitter—the insane. I have known others who were gentle and kind. Judging men becomes a kind of instinct after a while. A man knows those who can kill and those who cannot."

Cannon murmured resignedly, "I don't doubt your sincerity. But you're wrong." He was cold, as though by coldness alone he could turn aside the priest's persuasiveness. "How did you find me, by the way?"

The priest brightened. "Another argument that there must be something good in your father. His friends. There are two of them who have stuck by him all these years, coming to see him, writing to him. It was through one of these that he learned your whereabouts."

Cannon stirred restlessly. Father Gonzales began to talk hurriedly, anxiously, "Your father knew you hated him. He thinks you still hate him. He had learned to live in prison, had learned to bear its unbearable monotony. But he never learned to bear the thought of his only son hating him. Why do you suppose he risked his life to escape? Because he wanted to be free? Because he wanted to clear his name?" The priest shook his head. "Not for any of these things, but for something quite different. He wanted to regain the respect of his son. He wanted to make you stop hating him."

Cannon was silent, his face somber.

Obviously encouraged, the priest went on. "He will not let himself be captured, Mr. Cannon. He will not allow himself to fail at this last task he has set for himself. He will fight like a wolf if they catch up with him. And then he will truly be a murderer. As for learning anything . . ." He shrugged. "The sheriff in Red Butte has been notified to watch for him. A man has been dispatched from the prison to Red Butte to assist the sheriff. A third man will follow you when you leave here tonight."

Cannon muttered resignedly, "Just what is it you want me to do?" He had no enthusiasm for this, and his manner plainly showed it. It also showed a certain fatalism, as though he had known all along that in answering the priest's summons he was committing himself to do whatever it was the priest wanted him to do.

"Go to Red Butte. Find your father before the law finds him. Persuade him to give himself up and take upon yourself the task he has set for himself."

"How can I, when I don't believe in it?"

Father Gonzales smiled confidently. "Go to Red Butte and at least find your father and talk to him. In the meantime, try to remember what your father was like before the tragedy. If he was good to you, remember that. Try to give him the benefit of the doubt, to forget what he is supposed to have done."

Cannon grinned sourly and asked with considerable irony, "Is that all you want, Father?"

The priest replied soberly, "That is all," ignoring the irony. "Will you do it?"

Cannon shrugged, shaking his head with some puzzlement. "I don't know. I'll have to think on it."

He rose, shook the priest's frail hand, then opened the door and went through the dimly lighted church and out into the hot night air.

Automatically he fished in his pocket for tobacco and papers. The sounds of the night entered his ears but failed to register on his brain. He finished the cigarette but failed to light it, distracted momentarily by the sudden, soft strumming of the same idler's guitar.

How long he stood there before the Mission he did not know. He kept recalling the dim impressions of boyhood, the tobacco smell on his father's coat, the smell of horses. He remembered the little gifts of candy his father had sometimes brought him, and recalled being tossed high in the air by a black-bearded giant who laughed delightedly whenever the boy laughed. He even remembered going to sleep with his head on the rough woolen coat and wakening carefully tucked into his own bed.

Savagely he shook off these weakening

memories. In a minute he'd be drooling mawkishly about character and innocence and good and bad like that priest back there.

All right then. He'd go to Red Butte. But he didn't have to like it and he didn't have to believe in what he was doing. All he had to do was to save the old man's life.

Not from love, or duty, or even in respect. Not even because the priest had asked it so persuasively. But only because the old man was his flesh and blood—the last tie between himself and the old life—the one that had been so natural and so good.

In mid-afternoon of the third day, Stuart Cannon topped the crest of Comanche Pass and reined up in the timber to stare before him with a certain startled awe.

Below stretched the valley, bowl-shaped and nearly fifty miles long. The Giant's Graveyard, it was called, named for dozens of strange rock formations which rose like tombstones out of the valley floor and towered five hundred feet above it.

Each was a straight-rimmed pillar of red sandstone which tapered off into a brushy talus slope perhaps halfway down to the valley floor. They varied in shape, of course, and over the years each had been given a name. Red Butte. Seven Cities. Chimney Rock. Needle Rock. Elephant Rock.

Red Butte, the town, lay at the foot of Red Butte, the monument. Cannon's eyes picked it out from its remembered shape. It lay, perhaps fifteen miles away, straight out toward the center of the Giant's Graveyard, partly obscured by a thin dust-haze that lay unmoving across the vast valley.

He twitched his reins, raising the horse's weary, drooping head, and continued downward until he reached the level expanse of valley floor. Then, with Red Butte to guide him, he pointed his horse out toward its center.

Nostalgic memories, stirred by the sight of the Giant's Graveyard, crowded Cannon's consciousness as he rode along and brought, inevitably a return of his memory of that awful day, a return of bitterness.

He rode in a straight line, thoughtful and preoccupied, and near sundown found himself almost to the base of a monument called Chimney Rock and riding directly toward it.

Rather than detour its half-mile diameter, he rode up the talus slope on the eastern side, and at the top, backed by the bare, perpendicular face of rock, halted his horse to blow.

The sun, sinking toward the western horizon, had flooded the Giant's Graveyard with color. Red-orange tinged the bare faces of the towering monuments. Pink flowed across the sky. In the shadows behind the monuments, there was violet, deep gray-purple, and even a shade very close to green.

Movement on the valley floor caught Cannon's attention, and at once a more-than-passing interest stirred his face. He studied the rider below him briefly. Something else, further away, drew his attention, and he discovered another rider a couple of miles away, approaching at a quickened gallop.

He returned his glance to the first rider with some puzzlement since it was that one who was behaving most peculiarly. He seemed to have no definite destination. Instead, he was circling and intently watching something as yet unseen by Cannon in the center of his circle.

Unable for the moment to see what the rider was circling, Cannon studied the man himself. Even at a distance of a quarter-mile, he was plainly tall, plainly narrow-shouldered, and Cannon got the impression that he was rather on the unkempt side, although he could not have told why.

Cannon could not see his features at all, but he had another impression which was that the rider had something treed within that circle, something he had lately run to earth.

There was a rifle in the man's saddle boot, its stock rising beside the saddle horn on the left side, and he wore a cartridge-studded belt and holstered revolver.

Cannon fished for makings and rolled a cigarette thoughtfully. Curious, he continued to watch.

Suddenly he caught a flash of gray within the circle. Quite plainly the rider caught it at the same time, for instantly his revolver came out and fired.

*A wolf*, thought Cannon. And the man hadn't even noticed it. Flat and sharp, the report reached Cannon's ears.

The gray shape faded from brush clump to brush clump, a shadow seen by Cannon only because of his greater elevation, but obviously unseen now by the rider who left his circle's perimeter and advanced toward its center at a gallop.

Cannon's forehead furrowed with puzzlement. How did it happen that the rider had managed to run a wolf to earth in country such as this? It should have been ridiculously simple for the wolf to elude him, and the animal showed no signs of being wounded.

Even now, the wolf showed no inclination to run in a straight line, but continued to elude the rider by circling.

And then, quite suddenly, the rider did something strange. He returned his revolver to its holster and took down his rope.

*Is he going to try roping that wolf?* wondered Cannon in unbelief.

But it was becoming apparent that the rider could no longer see the wolf. It was becoming obvious that there was something else in the center of that circle. For the rider took a direct path to the center and his rope went out.

At a distance of over a quarter-mile, Cannon heard a squawl. There was a brief flurry of movement at the end of the rope. He heard the rider's laugh, taunting, cruel.

Cannon could see, at last, what the rider had caught. A man, an incredibly ragged, bearded man with gray hair that reached below his shoulders. A man with bare feet who whimpered and squawled like a wild thing, who fought the rope with insensate fury.

Recognition struck Cannon's memory like a blow. He knew the wild man, knew him from childhood.

He reined over unthinkingly and spurred down the slope. He had seen this cruel game played out before, though never quite so savagely, and never by grown men. He had even been a part of it once, and the memory of that stirred obscure shame in him.

Now, as he rode, doubt touched him briefly, and he questioned the wisdom of interference but his doubt vanished before the continuous, animal-like squawls of the roped wild man.

# Chapter III
## Man and Girl

Philippe Benoit. His story was legend in the Giant's Graveyard. Half owner of the sprawling Singletree ranch, he had turned to a hermit's existence years and years ago after the death of his wife and infant child in the space of a few short months. Some said he had lost his mind.

He lived in a tiny, one-room shack out in

the middle of Singletree range, lived with his wild pets and if anyone approached, he'd flee into the brush, as timid as a deer.

As Cannon drew closer, he studied the man who held the rope's end. Wholly pre-occupied with his cruelty, this man had no notice for anything but his helpless victim and did not see Cannon at all. He kept spilling Benoit, dragging him, laughing his high, thin, cruel laugh.

Cannon's first impression of the man had been largely correct. He was tall, gangling and narrow-shouldered. Unkempt too. His hair curled untidily at his neck and was long enough on both sides to almost completely cover his ears. His face was covered with a week-old stubble of mouse-colored whiskers. His nose was thin, with rather large, flaring nostrils. His lips were full, almost colorless, and slack and loose, twitching constantly.

Memory prodded Cannon as he watched the man, who suddenly looked up and met his gaze.

Cannon started. "Well, for Judas' sake! Turk! Billy Turk!"

Puzzlement touched Turk's wild, unstable eyes. Cannon said with patent disgust, "Hell, I'd think you'd have outgrown this. Turn him loose."

177

He was unprepared for the violence which flared in Turk's eyes. And he saw no recognition of himself there.

At the end of the rope, Benoit gained his feet and clawed at the loop. Turk's glance flicked to him and he reined his horse aside to spill Benoit again.

But Cannon was in the way. Deliberately he had ridden up on Turk's side and he stood his ground as Turk's horse collided with his own.

He was prepared for a fight, he was even ready if Turk had chosen to draw his gun. Instead, Turk did the unexpected. With a wild-eyed glare at Cannon, he sank spurs into his horse's sides.

The horse leaped out, in a full, hard run before he had covered a dozen yards. The rope jerked cruelly tight, dallied as it was to Turk's saddle horn.

Benoit screamed as the loop cut into his flesh, as the tightened rope yanked him off his feet. He fell into a clump of sagebrush, caught on its tough, twisted trunks and flopped free like a rag doll.

Thought was not conscious in Cannon, but he was aware that Benoit would be a bloody, dead thing in a matter of seconds if something were not done.

The motion that brought his gun clear was automatic. It leveled and barked. He holstered it and sank his own spurs even as Turk's horse faltered.

Dust raised in a cloud from Benoit's limp body. Dust raised from the hooves of Turk's horse. The animal's head went down and his front legs collapsed beneath him.

With a saddleman's instinct, Turk's feet kicked free of the stirrups and his body went limp and relaxed. As the horse fell, he flung himself clear, aided by the horse's own forward catapulting movement.

He landed a dozen feet away, head first in a clump of brush.

Recognizing the extreme danger that Turk would present once he collected his senses and gained his feet, Cannon kept going and jumped, running, from his saddle while he was yet twenty feet from the wildly struggling Turk.

Turk fought the brush savagely, trying to gain his feet, and he did while Cannon was still half a dozen feet away. Instantly Turk's hand flashed toward his gun.

Cannon hit him with all the drive of his running body behind the blow. He could almost feel Turk's nose split, and blood spurted out as suddenly as though Cannon had smashed a ripe tomato.

Turk lifted clear of the ground, went over the brush clump and landed behind it. When he came up, his eyes were blinded with tears and his nose streamed a crimson flood.

Cannon scrambled around the brush clump and sank his fist in Turk's belly, getting a kind of savage pleasure from the grunt that escaped Turk's twisted mouth.

He grabbed Turk's right wrist and whirled the tall man around with a vicious twist. He yanked Turk's gun from its holster and thrust it into his own belt. Then with a certain disgust, he flung the whimpering Turk away from him.

Breathing hard, he retraced his steps to the place where Turk's horse lay, utterly still on his side. He withdrew the rifle from the saddle boot, jacked the cartridges out into his hand, then flung the rifle into a thick clump of brush. He put the cartridges into his pocket.

With the wild flare of action over, he stood still for an instant, breathing hard. His knees trembled slightly and he could feel the nerves jumping all through his body. He remembered Benoit.

The brush was high here, higher than a

man's head. He could not see Benoit from where he stood, but he could see his horse— and another horse that had not been there a moment ago.

He remembered the rider he had seen approaching at a gallop, and came around the clump of brush with a tense readiness within him.

He relaxed instantly as he saw a girl, bending over Benoit's limp body.

She heard him, and looked around, her eyes blazing with outrage.

She looked almost savage herself. Her glistening black hair tumbled across her face. Her dark eyes flamed. Her mouth twisted with anger.

Puzzlement touched her at once as she saw Cannon. "Who are you? I thought . . ."

"You thought it was Billy Turk? He's over there behind that brush with a bloody nose and a pain in his belly."

She seemed to forget him after that and turned back to Benoit.

The wild man's face was covered with brush scratches. His shirt had been torn almost off him, exposing a thick chest covered with gray hair. He was breathing, Cannon noticed.

The girl was wiping his face ineffectually with a scrap of white handkerchief. Cannon knelt and grabbed Benoit's wrist. The pulse was steady and strong. He examined the wild man's head, finding a rather nasty lump.

He became aware of an elusive perfume and looked up at the girl, whose face was no more than six inches from his own. "He'll come around in a minute. He's just knocked out."

"What happened?" Her eyes, so close to his, were wide, frightened, like the eyes of a startled doe.

Cannon settled back on his haunches. His hand moved automatically to his shirt pocket and he began to make a smoke. "Didn't you see it?"

She shook her head. "I was crossing a wash."

Cannon grinned tightly, "I saw Turk rope Benoit and start to drag him. I interfered. I knew Benoit wouldn't live long, so I shot Turk's horse."

The explanation seemed to satisfy her, but it did not kill the puzzlement in her eyes. "How did you know their names? You're a stranger."

Suddenly Cannon remembered this girl.

He said, "I'm no stranger. You're Eve Redfern, aren't you?"

She nodded, her bewilderment increasing. Cannon said, "I've been gone for a long time. I'm Stuart Cannon."

He could see that the name was familiar to her, as it would naturally be. He could also see that she did not remember him personally. He said, "I was only twelve when I left. That was after . . ."

She nodded vigorously. "I know. I remember now."

Her forehead was furrowed, and he knew she did not remember him. She only remembered the name, and the lurid scandal connected with it.

Benoit groaned, and her glance went instantly to him. The wild man opened his eyes, which were crazy with fear. They calmed when they touched the girl, and he even smiled very slightly. Eve said soothingly, "You're all right now. It's all over."

Benoit's beard was filled with dust and blood. His face was dirty. He struggled upright and squatted on his haunches. The vague blank look returned to his eyes, the look Stuart remembered so well. He stared at Eve, and Cannon, and got to his feet.

Cannon thought, *He's going to run. He's going to run away.*

But Eve caught Benoit's arm. "Let me take you home on my horse."

Benoit shook his head. He whirled and started to trot away. But his leg folded beneath him and he fell headlong.

Eve uttered a small cry. Cannon said, looking at Benoit's leg, "Twisted it. It doesn't look broken. But he won't walk home tonight."

He walked over and got Eve's horse. He led the horse to where Benoit waited, sitting up, and between them they helped Benoit into the saddle.

Cannon had, for a moment, forgotten Billy Turk. An uneasiness made him turn and he saw Turk, mopping his nose with a bandana, watching with vitriolic hatred. Cannon said harshly, "Start walking. You can come back for your saddle in the morning."

Turk didn't say anything. He was so wildly enraged that he couldn't. But his eyes promised Cannon many things, none of them pleasant. He turned and stalked away, limping slightly, in the direction of town.

Eve spoke behind Cannon's back. "He won't let Benoit alone. Every time he crosses

Benoit's trail, he follows it. Today, I just happened to notice Benoit's tracks with horse tracks following and I guessed that Turk was after him again."

So far, Benoit had not said a word. It was as though he were mute, as though he could not speak. He kept glancing from Eve to Cannon and back again in the way of a wild thing. Suddenly he reined aside and drummed on the horse's ribs with his bare feet. The horse broke into a gallop, and in an instant was out of sight, hidden from the two on the ground by high brush.

Cannon asked, "Will his wolf follow him home?"

She shook her head. "No. The wolf won't follow horse tracks. But he'll get home sometime tonight."

"You want to go back to town, or after your horse?"

"You mean you'd let me have yours?"

Cannon shook his head. "I didn't say that. You'll have to ride double."

She gave him a look that was filled with suspicion. He said shortly, "Never mind. I'll bring your horse to you here."

Before she could protest, he swung up and rode away, leaving her staring angrily after him.

He was vaguely angered himself. Why did women always have to think that every man they met wanted to get his hands on them? He'd only suggested riding double because it would save time and effort for everyone concerned. Now she could sit and wait until he was blamed well able to get back for her.

He picked up Benoit's trail without difficulty although the light was fading fast. And kicked his horse into a fast trot.

He thought he remembered where the Benoit cabin was, but it had been a long time since he'd been there and he knew there was a good chance of wandering around for hours without finding it. The simplest way then, was to follow Benoit.

He hurried along and as fast as the first star twinkled in the deep-gray sky, came in sight of the shack that Philippe Benoit called home.

## Chapter IV
## Lloyd Cannon

There was a lamp burning in the dilapidated shack, shining out through the open door.

Eve Redfern's horse stood motionless immediately in front of it, reins trailing.

Cannon wondered briefly, as he rode in, whether Benoit had a gun or not, but shrugged, knowing he'd have to chance that.

Fifty feet from the cabin, he hailed, "Benoit! I came for the horse!"

He had to grin as Benoit burst from the door, and limping noticeably, disappeared into the brush. From the direction Benoit had gone, Cannon heard a coyote bark.

Another of the old man's pets, he supposed, no wilder than the old man himself.

He reached the door, and would have simply snatched the trailing reins without dismounting except for the fact that he saw a man's booted feet and lower legs inside the cabin.

Curiosity touched him, for he could not imagine Benoit and anyone else sharing the cabin. He swung down from his horse and stepped inside.

A man lay face down on the filthy pile of blankets which was apparently Benoit's bed. Beside the man was an empty whisky bottle and the cabin reeked with whisky which had spilled from the bottle and onto the blankets. From a barred cage on the far side of the room, a bobcat snarled and spit as Cannon came in.

For an instant Cannon hesitated. Perhaps he might have turned and gone out. But at that instant he felt the vaguest sense of familiarity with the man on the floor.

The man was balding, and graying too. But his hair had once been black, and his head had once been shaved.

Cannon stooped, suddenly enraged, and seized the man's shoulder. He yanked savagely, and the man rolled over onto his back.

As he stood, staring down, the years of hatred, the years of bitterness came flooding back, until it was all Cannon could do to keep from flinging himself upon the man on the floor. He had never wanted to kick anything so much before in his life.

His face was white, terrible.

One of the man's boottops had been cut away and his ankle was red and scabbed where the leg-iron had been. His clothing was ragged and old, stolen no doubt from some Mexican hut near the prison.

There was no substance to his body, and the clothes hung upon it like sacks. His face was hollow, gaunt. He was drooling a little and his lips were slack, his mouth half-open. He was dirty, unshaven, possessed of an unhealthy skin tone, caused no doubt by his years inside the dark prison.

But he was Stuart Cannon's father. In spite of change, in spite of Stuart's memory of a black-bearded giant, this was the one. The illusion of great size had been caused by Stuart's own small size.

A growl began deep in Cannon's throat. "Damn you! You killed my mother in a drunken stupor, then you get out of jail and the first thing you do is go into the same kind of drunken stupor!"

He was hardly aware of his surroundings, of the unutterably filthy cabin, of the crouched bobcat, watching him with yellow, unblinking, hate-filled eyes, of the smaller cages and their contents of small animals.

For he was thinking of Father Gonzales, of all those fine words about love and honor. He was thinking that here was the man who had broken prison because he could not stand the thought of his son hating him— that here lay the man who had risked his life to prove he was not guilty of the crime he had been convicted of.

Drunk! Dead drunk!

Cannon's fists were clenched at his sides.

His whole body was trembling with re-pressed rage.

How long he stood thus he could not have said. He was unaware of time, of its passage. He was unaware of everything but the man who lay snoring at his feet.

Some small part of his mind asked, *Well, what are you waiting for? You came to catch him, didn't you? You've caught him, haven't you? It was easy, but it was only luck, because neither you nor anyone else would ever have thought to look for him here.*

Benoit must be one of the friends the priest had mentioned.

Cannon shook himself visibly. He felt al-most physically sick. He stooped, control-ling his revulsion with difficulty, and picked up the limp form on the floor. It seemed weightless in his arms, but there was no pity in him.

He carried the man out and flopped him across the saddle. Still unconscious, the man retched. Reaching up, Cannon looped the old man's belt over the saddle horn to hold him in place. He picked up the reins of Eve Redfern's horse and mounted his own ani-mal, settling himself behind the cantle on the horse's rump. The horse didn't like it, but Cannon held him with a harsh hand.

His eyes were bleak, but surprise touched them as Benoit came timidly from the darkness. Benoit asked worriedly in a cracked, scarcely understandable voice, "Where are you taking him?"

"Red Butte. Jail."

Benoit plainly wanted to protest, but the timidity of the wild was too strong in him, and besides there must have been something about Stuart Cannon's eyes and still face which stopped him.

Cannon reined around and rode away.

His thoughts were not pleasant, nor was his expression. Strong by necessity himself, he had no real understanding of weakness in others. He could not understand, for instance, how a man who has once depended on liquor could crave it, even after ten years without it.

Cannon had never liked the stuff himself. He distrusted its effect on the sharpness of his mind, the sureness of his judgment. And he didn't like its taste. It gagged him.

Perhaps there was also a psychological distrust of liquor in him because of its responsibility for the wreckage of his life.

Here, before him, was an example of what

liquor could do to a man. In the saddle before him, Lloyd Cannon stirred, and groaned, and dry-retched again.

Full dark came down upon the land as Cannon retraced his way to where he had left Eve Redfern, guiding himself by the towering silhouette of Chimney Rock.

He rode to within a hundred yards of where he had left her, and was halted by her hail, which made no attempt to conceal her anger and irritation. "Stuart? Over here."

He turned and rode directly to her. Without speaking, he handed the reins of her horse down to her. She made no attempt to mount, in spite of the impatience that had been in her hail. She was looking at the burden in Cannon's saddle, and at once a deep, frightened concern touched her voice, "Is he . . . was he hurt worse than we thought?"

Cannon said harshly, "This isn't Benoit. This is my father, Lloyd Cannon. He's drunk, Miss Redfern. Dead drunk. I'm taking him to Red Butte to jail."

"Where was he? Where did you find him?"

"In Benoit's cabin."

A certain incredulity touched her voice.

"And you're going to turn him over to the law? Just like that?"

"It's what I came here for."

"But he's your own father! He risked his life to escape from prison. Aren't you even going to wait until he comes to and talk to him? Don't you care why he escaped? Don't you even care to know why his freedom was so important to him?"

Cannon laughed coldly. "I know what he claimed was his reason for coming here. He claimed he was innocent. He was going to find out who really killed my mother." There was a world of bitterness in Cannon. At the moment there was only bitterness— nothing else. "But he didn't believe it enough to stay off the bottle. So now he's going back to prison."

Eve Redfern hesitated for a moment, then mounted her horse. Cannon said, "Lead out. I'll follow," and she did, wordlessly.

For a while they rode in silence. Finally Eve said, "You give me the shivers. How can a man be so cold, so heartless? Do you hate him that much?"

"I don't hate him at all. I stopped hating him a long time ago."

"Then why . . . ?"

Cannon said flatly, contemptuously, "He killed my mother. Am I supposed to respect him after that? How strong do you think the ties of blood should be? I told you I didn't hate him, and I don't. I just don't have any use for him. I don't want to see him and I don't want to think about him. I let myself be talked into coming here because the priest at the prison was afraid he'd be killed before he'd let himself be captured." Cannon laughed mockingly. "A kid could have taken him."

"Have you considered that your father might be telling the truth?"

Cannon growled impatiently, "You were a child when it happened. You don't remember. He was drunk that night just like he is right now. He didn't remember a thing. He didn't know whether he did it or not. But a jury said he did and they sent him to prison for life. He spent over ten years in prison. Then, all of a sudden, he decides he isn't guilty. So he escapes." He stopped and then said shortly, "I don't want to talk about it."

Eve was silent for a while, but at last she said, "I remember you now. I think the reason I didn't before was that you'd changed so much. You're not the Stuart

Cannon I knew. You've spent your life brooding and hating until. . . ." She groped for words, angrily, "Maybe you have stopped hating your father. But you hate everything else instead. You hate the world and the people in it."

"Do I now?" Cannon's own anger was on the rise.

"Yes you do."

Cannon could not understand his own defiance. "And why shouldn't I? I've had to fight for . . ." He stopped, chagrined at the way he had so nearly been drawn out. This girl would not understand his bitterness. She had no idea of what it was to fight for each mouthful of food, to be cold and hungry. She could never understand a boy's wish to be accepted, a wish forever answered with suspicion and abuse. She could not know how eventually a shell formed as a defense against that. A hard, impenetrable shell, so that the kicks and blows could not hurt so deeply.

Suddenly he wanted this to be over with—finished. He wanted to be away from this girl, wanted to be rid of the inert burden in the saddle before him. He withdrew into a shell of taciturnity, answering her conversational attempts with curt monosyllables, until at last she gave up angrily.

Thereafter they rode in complete silence, until the lights of the town winked at them through the darkness.

To Stuart, riding in, the town seemed much smaller than it once had. The buildings seemed shabby, and the Southwestern Hotel, once so grand a structure in his eyes, was only an ornate, rather small two-story building badly in need of a coat of paint.

There was an odd, unpleasant feeling in his stomach as they passed the livery barn, so vivid did its unchanged appearance stir his memory. He said, "Is the jail still in the same place—a block south of the livery barn?"

"Yes." She reined in beside him and studied him. He found her regard disconcerting, and looked away. She said, "Won't you reconsider? Won't you wait and talk to him?"

"No." He didn't like uncertainty and he didn't like doubt. He liked things simple and uncomplicated, even his own thoughts and emotions. You were hungry, and you ate. You were tired, and you slept. You craved the company of a woman and you found one, but not one who would try to confuse you and make something binding and complicated out of it.

Talking to his father could accomplish nothing.

He did not tell Eve Redfern good-bye. He simply reined over and headed for jail.

## Chapter V
## Eve Redfern

Eve Redfern watched him go. There was considerable anger in her expression. She could not recall meeting a man who angered her so instantly, who kept feeding the anger within her so continually.

*He's not a man,* she told herself. *He's a block of stone.*

Yet she knew, even as she thought it, that it was not true. He had simply built a wall of stone around himself and it was, perhaps, natural that the wall offered a not-to-be-refused challenge to Eve.

Walls were made to be breached.

She saw him rein in before the lamplighted window of the sheriff's office, saw him shift the inert man in the saddle to his shoulder and stride to the door. She turned her head away, frowning in a troubled way.

Eve Redfern was a beautiful girl. She was accustomed to being treated as such. This was a land filled with working men, with fighting men, and there were not enough women to go around.

It was not that Eve was vain. Actually she did not even enjoy the eager attention shown her by most men. But Stuart Cannon's cold indifference, by its very novelty, both intrigued and annoyed her.

Her horse stood patiently for a moment, and when Eve did not move, stirred and headed for the hotel automatically out of long habit. Eve let him go, reins back.

She was a small, slight girl, filled with a boundless, nervous kind of energy. It showed itself in her quick, clean movements, so like the prancing of a high-spirited horse. It showed itself in the things she did to dissipate it—the long rides, the violence of her home activity when at times she would clean the entire house in a single day.

When she baked, she filled the kitchen with her baking, and spent the following two days riding hither and yon giving it away to families in need. When she sewed, she did not rest until she had finished whatever it was she had started.

She was hard on horses because she was

impatient, because in driving a horse, she was, in a way, driving herself.

Most times, in spite of her father's objections, she wore a split riding skirt of a length that would be considered scandalous in any but John Redfern's daughter, and a small-size man's plaid shirt, the brighter the better. Her hair was long, an inky, silken mass, whose tumbling confusion so annoyed her that she wore it tied behind her head with a bright ribbon.

No amount of sun seemed able to darken her smooth, ivory skin, and the only evidence of her exposure to it was a small bridge of golden freckles across her nose. Her eyes were the green of jade, yet they had none of the coldness so common in green eyes.

She resembled in no way the blond giant who was her father. And this was sometimes puzzling to her.

The town was rather quiet tonight. Riding along, she spoke to two or three people she passed, and their voices, answering, were friendly. She kept seeing that still, wary face of Stuart Cannon. She kept wondering what thoughts were behind its carefully controlled lack of expression.

Her anger came back, but this time, strangely enough, it was anger at herself rather than at him. *Forget him,* she told herself impatiently. *He's done what he came to do and he'll probably be gone before morning. You'll not see him again—and a good thing, too. He's unpleasant and cold, and probably a trouble-maker as well.*

She dismounted at the hotel steps. From the veranda a Singletree puncher came and took her reins. She murmured, "Thanks, Dutch," smiled at him and went on up the steps. Behind her, Dutch called in a softly warning voice, "*Viel Glück, Fräulein.* You vill need it. Your father has been for you vaiting already two hours."

She entered the tile-floored lobby and found him instantly with her glance. At the sound of the door, his ponderous head swung toward her.

He was scowling and red-faced. His hair was a good deal like a lion's mane, and there were times when his face had its own odd resemblance to that of a lion. This was one of those times. His pale eyes seemed to blaze at her.

She went to him and said quickly, "Father, Billy Turk was after Philippe again. He roped him and was dragging . . ."

"I've told you not to ride after dark."

She ignored that. "Father, guess who's in town after all these years." She was desperately trying to divert his thoughts from herself. Not because she feared his anger but because she wished to avoid a scene here in the lobby.

He growled disinterestedly, aware that he was being purposely diverted, "Who?"

"Stuart Cannon. I haven't seen him since he was twelve. His father broke out of prison and was staying at Benoit's place." Breathlessly, she launched into a narrative of all that had happened that afternoon, accounting for her being late, and ending up with Stuart's delivery of his father to jail.

"His father has come to the conclusion that he didn't . . . well, kill Stuart's mother. He came back to try to prove it. I think it's awful to haul him to jail, but maybe if Stuart talks to him he will believe in him too and try to get to the bottom of it for him."

She saw that she had succeeded in diverting her father's thoughts from her lateness. His anger had faded and the flush it had caused was gone from his face. He busied himself with a cigar which he took from the breast pocket of his coat. He unwrapped it and bit off the end. When he spoke, his voice was calm, almost without expression, "That's a sordid story for a young girl to be thinking about. You'd better forget it." He took her elbow. "Come on. I'm starving."

Eve could feel his hand trembling against her arm, but he seemed to have forgotten entirely her lateness and his anger because of it.

Usually he held her chair for her in his ponderously gallant way, but tonight he did not. Ruth Layton, the waitress, came at once with her deferent, "Good evening, John. What will it be tonight?"

And only after John Redfern had given his order did Ruth look at Eve. "Hello, Eve. You want the same thing?"

Eve nodded. Redfern said, "Hurry it, Ruth. We're already late."

"Of course." Ruth hurried away, a thin, springy woman of middle age who never quite managed to conceal the adoration she felt for John Redfern but who never for a moment forgot its futility.

Eve noticed that her father still held the cigar, unlighted, in his hand. As she watched, he tucked it absently back in his pocket.

She asked, "Are you worried about something, Father?"

"Worried?" He shed his preoccupation instantly. "Of course not. Why should I be worried?"

"I don't know, but . . ."

"Nonsense." He looked around the room. "Where the devil is Ruth. I'm hungry."

Ruth came threading through the tables, bringing their supper, and Eve attacked hers at once with a healthy, girlish hunger. She was not quite finished when John Redfern rose. "I have some things to do, Eve. I'll see you later."

He rose, smiled at her absently and left the room. Eve glanced across at his plate and discovered that he had scarcely eaten a bite, in spite of his earlier statement that he was starving.

A puzzled frown drifted across Eve's smooth forehead.

## Chapter VI
## John Redfern

Upon leaving the dining room, John Redfern went out onto the hotel veranda. He fished the unlighted cigar from his pocket and studied it thoughtfully before putting it between his teeth and lighting it.

Dutch Vosmer, still idling in one of the cane chairs, spoke to him softly, "Evenin', Mr. Redfern," and Redfern nodded.

Redfern stood there for almost ten minutes. Then, suddenly, his abstraction vanished and he said, turning toward Vosmer, "Dutch, find Billy Turk and tell him I want to see him."

"Sure, Mr. Redfern." Dutch's voice, while courteous, showed no particular enthusiasm. Redfern turned and went into the hotel. He climbed the stairs to the small suite of rooms which was his home in town, and without removing his hat, crossed to the writing desk and sat down.

He selected a sheet of paper, and with a pencil, began to print carefully on it. When he had finished, he folded the paper, slipped it into an envelope and sealed it. On the face of it, he carefully printed the name of the addressee.

He had scarcely finished when someone knocked on the door. Redfern stuck the envelope into his side coat pocket before he called, "Come in."

Turk came in. He held his hat in his hands, and his face was a mass of brush scratches. His nose, normally straight and narrow, was swelled painfully, twisted, and varied in shaded from purple to a dull green-black. Redfern said, "I thought I told you to leave Benoit alone."

Turk's eyes flared. He didn't answer. His lips quivered sullenly and one corner of his mouth twitched. His eyes were bulbous, protruding, and one of them was slightly crossed.

Redfern did not make an issue of Benoit, being aware that he could no more keep Turk away from Benoit than he could keep a house cat away from a mouse. Instead, he said quietly, "There's something I want you to do. I want it done right and I don't want anyone to know you did it."

Turk made an obvious effort to turn his thoughts from their own channels, and in the attempt, grinned rather vacantly and foolishly. Redfern said sharply, "If you're caught, it's your problem, understand? Blab and you won't live to blab a second time."

Turk's grin faded before Redfern's intensity. Redfern studied him a moment. Turk was savage and vicious and he wasn't overly bright. It was always hard to tell what Turk might do. But there was a tenacious loyalty in him toward Redfern and Singletree, a loyalty which Redfern had inspired over the years by always getting Turk out of the scrapes his viciousness got him into. Redfern was reasonably sure he could count on Turk's loyalty in anything.

He said, "There's a man over in the jail—Lloyd Cannon—the father of the man you had your run-in with." Turk scowled, and licked his lips, puzzled apparently at what this was all leading up to.

Redfern opened the desk drawer and took out a small, nickel-plated .38. He said, "This gun can't be traced to me. I want Cannon to have it."

He saw the instant refusal in Turk's eyes and his own glance hardened. He said, "This is going to hurt young Cannon worse than anything else you could do to him. Take my word for it."

"But how—?"

"How are you going to get it to him? Very easy. You know that old woodshed behind the livery barn? Well, there's going to be a fire there in about an hour. It's almighty close to the livery barn, and if the livery barn goes up the whole town will too. Everybody knows that, and everybody in town will turn out to fight the fire."

He smiled a little. "There's no one in the jail but this Lloyd Cannon, and he's dead drunk. You be where you can watch the jail door. The sheriff's got an extra set of keys in the top left-hand drawer of his desk. Unlock Cannon's cell and slip the gun down inside his belt where he can't fail to find it. Then get out and don't forget to lock the cell door behind you."

He could see questions forming in Turk's slow mind, but he gave Turk no time to formulate them. He said, "Don't forget, now. And no more drinking until you've done what I told you."

Turk nodded. He turned his hat around a couple of times in his hands, shuffled his feet and cleared his throat. But in the end he decided against questioning Redfern and turned to the door. He went out without looking back, and Redfern crossed the room and closed the door.

He sat down, outwardly calm, and waited. He went over his plan in his mind, carefully scrutinizing it for flaws. If all went as he had planned it, Cannon would get the gun. The man from the prison would get the anonymous, printed note in Redfern's pocket.

Sometime tomorrow, when his hangover

had worn off enough so that he could think, Cannon would make his break. The man from the prison, warned, would be watching. He wouldn't know what he was up against, one man or a dozen. So when Lloyd Cannon ran out with a gun in his hand, the man would shoot him down.

No one would know how Cannon got the gun. And with the old man dead, it was certain that his son would saddle up and ride on.

Pleased with himself, and smiling slightly, Redfern got to his feet.

He went downstairs, through the lobby and out to the street. Dutch Vosmer was sitting again in the cane chair near the door. Dutch didn't drink, so there was little he could do when he came to town except sit here and watch the town pass before his eyes.

Redfern nodded to him and strolled down the street.

He often took walks after dinner, and he knew that unless he was seen, no one would think to connect him with the fire. He took his time, stopping frequently to talk politics or weather or the state of the cattle business with some acquaintance.

But three-quarters of an hour after leaving the hotel, he was a block beyond the livery barn, and for once was by himself.

He stopped and lighted another cigar. He puffed on it contentedly while he scanned the street. Satisfied that no one was noticing him, he turned unhurriedly off Main and headed for the alley that ran behind the livery stable.

He walked along it quietly but making no obvious effort to conceal himself. He came to the small shed and eased open the squeaking door.

Split firewood was racked up neatly along one wall. Along the other wall were sacks of grain and perhaps a dozen bales of spoiled hay which the stableman could not feed but would not throw away.

Careful of his clothes, Redfern yanked the wires off one bale and scattered its contents carefully about the shed. He laid a narrow trail of hay from the pile to the door and paused there to look at what he had done.

It was very dark, but not so dark that he could not see. Satisfied, he thumbed a match alight and dropped it at the end of the hay trail in the doorway. Before it could catch and make a noticeable flare, he stepped outside and closed the door behind him.

He returned along the alley by the way he had come, and went back to Main, hurrying just a little now. There was one more thing to do.

It worked out precisely as he had hoped it would. He was just entering the hotel as he heard the first shout.

He crossed the lobby and climbed the stairs. Outside, the bell in the church steeple began to clang frantically. Doors along the hallway opened, their tenants looking out, and a man asked, "What's going on?"

Redfern said, "Sounds like a fire alarm." He went quickly to his room, but he did not close the door. He could hear the hotel emptying, could hear the commotion in the street that always went with a fire. Fire was a terror to the people of a small town, because there was never any telling where it would stop.

He saw the man who had been sent from the prison pass his door, and this was what Redfern had been waiting for. Quickly he returned to the hall, closing his door behind him. The man, running, turned the corner at the end of the hall and disappeared.

Redfern took the envelope he had prepared from his pocket. He went along the hall until he came to the man's room, and stooping, slipped it under the door. Straightening, he looked down the hall to be sure no one had seen him.

Then, smiling in an extremely satisfied way, he broke into a run himself, heading for the stairs.

He'd fight the fire with the rest of them, and he knew there'd be no particular difficulty in putting it out. The shed was small, and there were half a hundred fire fighters.

But the fire would have served its purpose and there would be no one to point a finger at John Redfern. Except Turk and Turk knew better than to spill anything he knew.

## Chapter VII
## Rigged

Stuart Cannon had just entered his hotel room when the fire broke out. He went to the window and peered down into the street. At once his glance found the glare, and he knew that the fire was in the little shed behind the livery barn.

How many times had he stood beside that

shed, splitting wood and carrying it inside? How many times had he wished it would burn down? He smiled a little, remembering.

He considered going downstairs to help, but realized at once that there were too many fire fighters as it was. They'd be getting in each other's way without any help from him.

Yet an odd restlessness possessed him tonight so he put on his hat and went out into the hall. The last of the hotel's tenants were pouring down the stairs as he reached them, and he recognized the ponderous shape of John Redfern ahead of him.

Redfern had aged somewhat in the time Stuart had been gone. There was a silvery sheen to his yellow hair that had not been there when Stuart left. Otherwise he seemed much the same, huge, confident, arrogant. The big man of the communtiy.

Cannon descended into the lobby and went to the big plate-glass window to stare into the street. Only a part of his mind was upon the confusion there, the remainder being upon the thing he had done this evening, upon his father sleeping it off in one of the jail's aseptic-smelling cells.

There was no reason, he told himself,

why he should feel so guilty. He had done what he agreed to do. He had kept his father from fighting to escape capture, perhaps had even saved his life.

But he also realized that he had not done quite all the priest had asked him to do.

This, then, was behind his feeling of guilt. He crossed the lobby and sat down.

Eve Redfern came into the lobby from the veranda. Apparently she had been watching the excitement from there, for her face was flushed, her eyes sparkling. She glanced at him, hesitated, and then came toward him. "Aren't you going to the fire?"

He shook his head. "Too many now. They don't need me."

Her eyes mirrored her instant thought, *And you don't need them.*

Cannon felt anger stir, so obvious was her thought, but he said nothing. Eve sat down on the leather-covered sofa beside him, perching on its edge. She asked, "Are you going to stay in Red Butte?"

He shook his head. "I've done what I came to do."

Eve's eyes flashed dangerously. She made a determined effort to control herself. "Where will you go?"

213

He looked at her without friendliness. "Back where I came from. Colorado."

"A ranch?" she probed.

He shook his head with exaggerated patience. "I've been trapping wild horses on the Colorado-Utah border. In two years I've put enough aside to buy myself a small herd of cattle. In another two years I'll have enough to buy a ranch to run them on. Is that what you wanted to know?"

"There's no need to be so unpleasant about it."

Cannon wondered what it was about the two of them that always managed to make the sparks fly. *Steel against flint*, he thought, but that didn't satisfy him either, for there seemed to be no hardness about this girl.

She said, "You'll never be quite satisfied unless you talk to your father. You realize that, don't you?"

She put to words the thing that had been bothering him. He knew that what she said was true.

He said, reluctantly and sourly, "All right. I'll talk to him, if it'll make you feel any better."

She stared at him and then got up. Her voice was level, tight. "Right now I don't care what you do. I was right this afternoon.

You may not hate your father, but you hate the world and everyone in it." She seemed about to say more. She seemed about to launch into a tirade. She controlled herself with difficulty and flounced angrily away. She ran up the stairs, and disappeared from sight.

Cannon sat quite still, his eyes smoldering. He did not like the confused state of his feelings. He did not like the way Eve Redfern could upset him.

She was a beautiful, vital woman and as such stirred certain earthy desires in him. These he had felt before and they were familiar and well understood. Yet the things she made him feel were more complex, and troubled him because he did not understand them.

Another man, confused and troubled as was Stuart Cannon, might have left the hotel, found a saloon, and proceeded to get roaring drunk. He'd have gotten himself into a good fight, and upon waking in the morning, would have felt released, and calm again. No such release was possible for Cannon, feeling as he did about liquor.

Moodily he rose and climbed the stairs to

his room. He went to bed, but it was past midnight before he slept.

As always, he awoke early. He got up, dressed, and walked to his window to stare outside. The monuments of the Giant's Graveyard were visible, and the rising sun stained their eastern faces a brilliant pink.

Nostalgic memory stirred in Cannon, and the almost forgotten feelings of boyhood came back. He remembered the sharp, friendly aroma of coffee, the small sounds his mother made moving about in the kitchen, the promise and challenge that each bright new day could offer a twelve-year-old boy. He remembered the feeling of belonging, of not being alone.

Not often did these memories return, but when they did, their pain was almost physical.

For the briefest instant, his remote eyes were soft, his still face expressive with loneliness. Then he remembered his father, and the jail, and his promise to visit and talk to him before leaving today.

The wary look returned to his eyes, the brooding expression to his face. He washed and shaved quickly, then stuffed his belongings into his leather saddlebags and left the room. He paid his bill at the desk and went into the dining room.

So early, the place was nearly deserted. In silence he ate his breakfast and rising, went out into the cool morning air.

He had left his horse at the livery barn with a boy of perhaps fifteen. This morning, the boy was gone, and the grossly fat livery man Cannon remembered came from the tack room as he opened the door.

Odd, how things never changed. Cannon cringed inwardly at the impact of the man's unpleasant little eyes. It was almost as though time had rolled back and he was again a boy, entering here for his daylight to dark stint of cleaning stalls and currying horses. He wanted to sink his fist into the stableman's fat midriff.

He said, "At least you haven't changed, have you, Dawson?"

The man made a bewildered effort to remember him. Cannon said, "Stuart Cannon, blame you. I promised myself at least a hundred times that when I was big enough I'd take a strap to you the way you used to do to me."

Fear touched Dawson's eyes, and he took

217

a backward step and laid his hand on the handle of a pitchfork. "Don't try it, Stuart."

Cannon laughed harshly. "Shut up and get my horse."

Motionless, Dawson stared at him, but in the end his glance wavered and fell away. Cannon said, "Chestnut gelding. Fifth stall on the wall from the back door."

Dawson stumbled away. After a few moments he brought Cannon's horse. Stuart Cannon flung up his saddle and cinched down. He could not resist flipping Dawson a silver dollar and turning away without waiting for change. He led the horse out, mounted and rode away without a backward glance.

He knew he had acted childishly, but found that he didn't feel much differently about Dawson than he had as a boy.

The sun was up now, and the streets were beginning to stir with life. Stuart Cannon reached the jail, and was swinging his leg over to dismount as he heard the shot. It came from inside the jail.

He froze, still in the saddle. A shot inside the jail could mean but one thing—a break. And Lloyd Cannon was the jail's only prisoner.

Across the street, a man who had been

lounging in the shadow of a cottonwood trunk stepped into the street, gun fisted. He had a lean, wary look to him with his flop-brimmed black hat and black coat. He looked like a manhunter. Stuart realized that the man's gun had more or less centered itself on him in the absence of a better target.

There was no further sound from inside the jail. Stuart swung from his horse and led the animal forward. Then he ducked around the horse and approached the door.

Lloyd Cannon, unshaven, dirty and wild of eye, flung it open and stepped onto the walk. In his hand he held a small, nickel plated revolver.

This puzzled Stuart Cannon. Why was that prison manhunter idling across the street this early in the morning, unless he had reason to believe there was going to be a break? Hell, the old man had darn near walked into a trap.

He looked up at his father, then down at the gun in his hand. He said, "Know me?"

His father's eyes were vague, frightened, trapped. The gun had swung immediately to cover him, but it had no real steadiness. Stuart said, "I found you out at Benoit's place and hauled you in here last night. If you're going to shoot me, get it over with."

"I couldn't shoot you, boy. Lord, you've changed." Lloyd Cannon's voice was a cracked whisper.

Behind him, Stuart could hear the shuffling steps of the prison manhunter coming closer. The pair was sheltered behind Stuart's horse, but it was a meager shelter at best. Stuart said, "Get back inside. There's a man from the prison in the street with a gun in his hand."

His father looked up, saw the man for the first time. His gun-hand dropped to his side and his shoulder slumped.

In the street, the manhunter's gun roared. The bullet smashed a window beside Stuart's head. He gave his father a shove and followed him inside.

With the heel of his boot, he kicked the door shut behind him. The sheriff sat in his swivel chair, tied and gagged. His eyes were virulent. Stuart walked over and removed the gag. He said, "Tell that damned fool in the street to quit shooting," but the sheriff only licked his lips and mouthed his tongue, trying to restore its moisture.

Lloyd Cannon seemed to be in a kind of daze. He still held the little revolver, but he had plainly forgotten it. He made a helpless and pathetic figure.

Stuart said, "Get back in your cell, Pa. You stepped into a rigged game. What beats me is who rigged it."

The sheriff hadn't said anything. Stuart cut the ropes from his hands and the sheriff stooped and yanked the hastily tied bonds off his feet. He got up and pushed Lloyd Cannon into a cell, first taking the nickel-plated revolver out of his hand. He locked the cell door and heaved a long sigh. "Judas! That was a devil of a thing to happen to a man so early in the morning."

The manhunter kicked open the door and burst into the room. The sheriff said, "Put that damned thing away. Everything's under control." He looked at the nickel-plated revolver, then at Stuart. "You slip him this?"

"No. And that's a stupid question. Would I haul him in to you last night when I didn't have to and then slip him a gun so he could get away again?"

"No, I guess you wouldn't." The lawman was tall, stooped, patient, his face wrinkled like old leather. Guy Kearns had been sheriff of Monument Country for twenty years, and was the man who had arrested Lloyd Cannon, who had testified against him at the trial. Stuart had always felt a kind of respectful awe in his presence and he still felt it.

Stuart was scowling. It was though he were in a long tunnel of utter darkness, as though he had always been in that tunnel. But right now, he could see the faintest glimmer of light ahead. He said, "Somebody slipped him that gun." He looked at the manhunter. "How'd you happen to be standing over there this early in the morning?"

The man fished an envelope from his pocket and handed it to the sheriff. Kearns read it and passed it to Stuart. Stuart read it and passed it back. He said, "Somebody is scared. Somebody wanted the old man killed as he tried to break jail. If that happened, I'd have ridden on and forgotten the whole thing."

Kearns said, "If I was you, I'd ride on anyhow."

"Huh-uh. Now I'm curious. I'd like to know who slipped him that gun. I'd like to know why. I'll stay 'till I find out."

The prison man said, "I'll start back with him this morning. There's a stage out at ten."

Stuart looked at him briefly then back to Kearns. He said, "Sheriff, I think you owe me something. I brought him in to you last night. I saved you a lot of riding, and maybe I saved you from dodging a few bullets. Make them extradite him."

The prison man started to say something, but Stuart cut him off. "Sheriff, you could have been shot because somebody slipped Pa a gun. Don't you want to know who did it?"

"How will keeping him here help?"

Stuart shrugged. "I don't know. But I'll bet that whoever it was knows something about my mother's death. If Pa's here to question, we'll get to the bottom of it a devil of a sight quicker."

Kearns looked at him sourly. He shrugged his thin shoulders and spoke with ill-concealed reluctance to the prison man. "Extradite him. I won't give him up."

The prison man began to argue with Kearns, but Stuart knew that once Kearns made up his mind nothing could change it. He walked over to the cell and looked at his father, surprised that for once he didn't feel anything in particular—no hate—no dislike—nothing. He asked, "Where'd you get the gun?"

Lloyd Cannon licked his lips. He rubbed

a hand over his unshaven face. "It was stuck in my belt when I woke up."

Kearns was watching Stuart closely as he turned. Kearns was hesitating about something, weighing him, but at last said, "You might learn things that you don't want to learn. Have you thought of that?"

Stuart stared at him incredulously. His anger leaped like a prairie fire. "What are you trying to say?"

"Well, when a woman is killed . . ." The sheriff didn't finish. Something he saw in Stuart's face seemed to close his throat. He swallowed with difficulty.

Stuart said harshly, "That's a man in that cell of yours. He's spent ten years of his life in a stinking prison. Are you suggesting that even if he isn't guilty I should let him go back and spend the rest of his life there?"

The years of bitterness and hatred had been bad enough, assuming that his father was guilty of his mother's murder. If he was not, they would have been for nothing. If Lloyd Cannon had not killed his wife, and someone else had, then the guilt of whoever had was truly appalling. Someone had to pay—for a woman's death, for a man's false imprisonment for ten years, for a boy's lifetime of bitterness and hardship.

224

There was a kind of craziness in Stuart Cannon. He stared wildly at the sheriff for a moment, then stalked hastily to the door. He had to think. He had to think.

Behind him the sheriff called out something he did not understand. He swung up on his horse and rode out of town at the wildest kind of run.

## Chapter VIII
## One Way

Stuart Cannon was not really aware of the horse under him, nor of the miles flowing past. He was not aware of the horse's exhaustion until the animal nearly fell while jumping a narrow wash.

Shamed, he pulled the horse in and dismounted. He took off the saddle and began to rub the lathered animal down with the saddle blanket.

But his mind wasn't on it.

His life as a man had begun when he was twelve, for it was then that he had been cut adrift. It had been nurtured on hatred, which had gradually faded to be replaced by a philosophy of withdrawal, of total self-sufficiency, of distrust of his fellow man.

Today, the foundations upon which he had built his life were crumbling. For if Lloyd Cannon were in truth innocent . . . He shook his head confusedly.

He became aware of the sound of a horse's hooves and looked up to see Eve Redfern gallop into sight. She rode directly to him and he knew she had been following him.

She started to dismount, but changed her mind. All her assurance seemed to vanish as she looked at his face. She asked timidly, "What happened? I heard that your father tried to break jail. I was heading for there when I saw you ride out. Your face was so terrible, I . . ."

He tried to concentrate his thoughts on Eve, but he did not really see her. Yet there must have been some softening in his expression for she dismounted and came to sit beside him. He dropped his head into his hands, covering his face and growing tense.

He sat this way for a long time. At last he shuddered and looked at her. He asked, "What if he didn't do it?"

"Do what? What are you talking about?"

He told her about the attempted jailbreak, about the revolver and about the anonymous note. He said, "That fire was set, last night. It was set to give someone a chance to get into the jail and put that revolver in my father's belt. Someone is scared. And now they'll be even more scared."

"What are you going to do?"

His eyes were terrible. "Find him, whoever he is."

"More hatred, Stuart? Suppose you're wrong. Isn't it possible that one of your father's friends, perhaps Benoit, got the gun to him?"

"Then how about the note?"

"Maybe someone saw Benoit or whoever it was go into the jail last night. Maybe they wrote the note rather than to become involved. Or perhaps they didn't want to accuse Benoit."

He looked at her steadily. "Do you believe that?"

She shook her head. "No. I don't believe it. But it's possible."

He had to admit that it was. And it was a steadying possibility. It eased the shock of such sudden and complete reversal of his beliefs.

Automatically he fished for tobacco and made himself a smoke. He lighted it and dragged the smoke deep into his lungs. He discovered that it was oddly comforting to have Eve here beside him.

He said bitterly, "If he isn't guilty, someone has a devil of a bill to pay."

She did not speak at once. When she did, her voice was soft, almost timid, "And what about the bill you owe, Stuart?"

He didn't pretend to misunderstand her. "Maybe I can pay part of it by finding the killer. I'll pay the rest after Pa gets out of jail."

He looked at her and there was a film of tears in her eyes. She whispered, "I'll help all I can."

"Why? Why should you want to help?"

She was instantly angry. Her eyes flashed and her lips tightened. She got to her feet and stood looking down. "Why do you have to be so darned suspicious? Why?" she mocked. "Why? Why? Do I have to have a reason except that you need help and I want to give it?"

He had never said, "I'm sorry" in his life, and he could not now. He stared at her, and she stared back, and dislike crept into her expression.

Without another word, she turned and mounted her horse. Looking down she said, "I'm sorry for you. Because there's something you just can't seem to learn."

"What's that?" He was angry, he discovered, as much at himself as at her.

"You get out of life exactly what you put into it. You get out of your relations with people exactly what you put into them. You have never put a single thing into either your life or your relations with other people. It's no wonder you've never gotten anything out."

His face stilled and his eyes blazed. Eve whirled her horse and rode away at a hard run, leaning low over her horse's withers, her midnight hair streaming out in the wind behind her.

In an instant she was gone from sight. Cannon stood up and kicked viciously at a sagebush clump. He was filled with a consuming, helpless rage.

He looked his horse over and discovered that the animal was breathing quietly, that his hide had dried and cooled. He saddled and mounted. He yanked his thoughts from Eve with an effort, and concentrated them on the problem which faced him. He realized that he faced a blank wall. He had been twelve when he left Red Butte. He could know nothing of the conflicts and problems which its inhabitants had faced. He could remember who had been here at the time and that was all.

Another thought occurred to him, and for an instant the helplessness faded from his face. Someone had engineered that jailbreak out of fear. The jailbreak had failed. Therefore, would not that someone's fear increase as a direct result of the failure? And would not their increased fear force still another move?

He decided that it would. He pointed his horse toward town, but now, he did not hurry, preferring instead to let his thoughts wander as they would.

John Redfern was in the hotel dining room with Eve when Dutch Vosmer came hurrying in with news of the jailbreak. His accent thickening with excitement, Dutch related all that had happened. Before he was through Eve got up and hurried from the room.

Redfern watched her go, trying hard to control the panic that clawed at his mind. He had not foreseen this. He had been a fool, but he had not foreseen failure.

He got up, partly to avoid Dutch's scrutiny of his face, and headed toward the lobby with Dutch walking beside him and talking excitedly.

230

Normally Red Butte was a dull town, enlivened only by the once-a-month antics of Singletree's punchers when payday came. In the past week, however, and particularly last night, enough had happened to keep the inhabitants supplied with excitement for months to come. Firstly, news of Lloyd Cannon's escape had come, immediately followed by the arrival of the manhunter from the prison.

Then Stuart Cannon had ridden into town with the old man draped across his saddle. This morning the jailbreak. No wonder Dutch was excited. Too excited, Redfern hoped, to notice the whitening of Redfern's face, the tremor that shook his hands.

He went through the lobby and out onto the veranda. He stared into the dusty street. He saw Stuart Cannon pound out of town as though pursued by the devil, and five minutes later saw Eve leave the same way. Dutch still talked brokenly and excitedly at his elbow and at last Redfern said, "Shut up, Dutch. You talk too much."

Abashed, Dutch fell silent.

Redfern had not felt panic such as he felt today for years. He had grown sure and confident with the passage of time and, he realized now, that very confidence had be-

231

trayed him. He had planned well last night, but he had not considered the possibility of failure. Now, Stuart Cannon would be suspicious, ready for the first time in his life to consider the possibility that his father was innocent of the crime of which he had been convicted.

But wait! Redfern frowned thoughtfully. Perhaps something could be salvaged out of the situation. Without too great a loss of prestige. Perhaps he might even be admired for what he had done.

He started to speak to Dutch, then changed his mind. He fished a cigar from his pocket and lighted it.

Stuart Cannon, he realized, still remained a problem. Unless . . . He turned abruptly to Dutch. "Go on out to the ranch. Get Tom O'Dell and bring him in. I want to talk to him."

Dutch looked puzzled, but he did not argue. He headed for the livery barn. Redfern puffed furiously on his cigar for a moment, then tossed it into the street and headed for the jail and the sheriff's office.

He could bring this off, he knew. For he was the other "friend" of which the priest had spoken to Cannon. He was the other man who had visited and written to Lloyd Cannon over the years.

The street was dusty, the sun warm against his back. He nodded briefly to Dawson, the stableman, who stood sweating and puffing beside the livery stable door. Dawson said breathlessly, "You heard about the jailbreak, Mr. Redfern?"

Redfern nodded. His nerves were jumping, but he guessed it wouldn't hurt if he showed a little nervousness at the sheriff's office. Anybody would be nervous, confessing complicity in a jailbreak.

He hesitated with his hand on the doorknob, then straightened his ponderous shoulders visibly and went in.

All was quiet now. The sheriff sat behind his desk. Back in the cell, Lloyd Cannon sat on his bunk, staring moodily at the floor. He looked as though he might have a headache, for he held his head in his hands.

Redfern cleared his throat. Guy Kearns looked up, his glance neither friendly nor otherwise. Neutral. He said, "Sit down, John."

Redfern sat down in the chair beside the sheriff's desk. He fished a cigar from his pocket, his hands shaking visibly. He said, "I guess I was wrong. When I think . . ."

Kearns' voice was flat. "What are you trying to say?"

"Guy, I was the one who arranged for Cannon to get that gun."

Genuine surprise touched Kearns' face. "But why? Why the devil would you do that?"

Redfern flushed and smiled, blending exactly the right amounts of humble shame and stubbornness in the smile. He felt just a little proud of himself. "I was Cannon's friend, Guy," he said simply.

He heard a stir of movement in the cell as Cannon got up and came to the bars. Redfern turned and said apologetically, "Lloyd, it never occurred to me you might be hurt."

Kearns said sourly, "And I'll bet it never occurred to you that Cannon might shoot me, either, did it?"

"I knew Lloyd wouldn't hurt you, Guy."

"Well, I wasn't so blamed sure when he put that gun on me this morning, shaky as he was!"

Redfern said, with an air of plunging in to unburden his conscience, "I set that fire in the shed to draw you out of the jail.

Then I sent Billy Turk into the jail to leave a gun with Cannon. I'll pay for the shed, sheriff. But I guess I'll have to stand trial, won't I?"

There was a world of humility in Redfern, and it was, perhaps this incongruous quality which seemed to confuse the sheriff. Kearns mumbled, "Well, I don't know. Let me talk to Dawson. I have an idea if he could make a nice profit on that shed he'd forget about preferring charges. But damn it Redfern, don't ever pull anything like that again. You ought to have your butt kicked,"

Redfern stood up. He went to the bars and looked at Cannon. "I'm sorry, Lloyd. I knew how bad you wanted to be free. I knew you wanted to try and clear yourself. I thought . . ." He left the sentence hanging. He could see that Cannon was tremendously moved.

He went out into the street. He was still shaking, but it was a pleasant thing now, the nervousness of intense relief. He'd pulled it off. He'd made it reflect to his credit. He had them eating out of his hand.

Behind him the sheriff yelled, "Hey!"

He turned, the fear crawling in him again. Kearns said, "Come back here!"

Redfern walked back to the jail. He hoped

he didn't look as panicky as he felt. But the sheriff's question relaxed him wonderfully. "What about the note?"

Relief sighed out of Redfern. He smiled. "Someone must have seen me, or Turk, or both of us. Maybe they didn't want to get involved, or maybe they just didn't want to accuse me. They used the note as a way out."

"A blamed dangerous way out, if you ask me," Kearns snorted. But the explanation seemed to satisfy him and he went back into his office, grumbling under his breath.

Redfern returned to the hotel, painfully conscious of the tight wire he was walking. One misstep, one error . . .

He thought, *I've got to work this out. I've got to get young Cannon out of town, one way or another. Because the longer he stays the more dangerous he'll become.*

There were, Redfern knew, some loose threads lying around. At any time, Cannon might happen upon one of them. There was Flora Curtice. There was Benoit.

Well, maybe Tom O'Dell would get rid of Cannon. At any rate, it was an angle worth trying.

Redfern entered the hotel and climbed the stairs to his rooms. He sat down beside the window and stared down into the street. Eve had not yet returned, probably would not for an hour or more. Redfern had no idea, of course, how far things had gone between her and Stuart Cannon. Not far, he judged. Still, it was obvious that Eve was attracted to Cannon. And if Cannon was not attracted to her he would be a fool.

At any rate, there was enough between them to feed Tom O'Dell's voracious jealousy. Redfern was willing to bet that when O'Dell was finished with him he'd be eager to leave Red Butte.

In a man like Redfern, confidence was renewed with each new plan. It was part of his monstrous ego. He began to smile, and thought, *That's a fight I wouldn't miss for anything*.

## Chapter IX
## The Fight

When Stuart Cannon got back to town, he went directly to the jail. His father was asleep in the cell, snoring softly. A young, fuzzy-cheeked deputy was holding down Guy Kearns' swivel chair, his feet on the desk. He looked up at Cannon, scowled and said. "What do you want?"

"Where's the sheriff?"

The deputy said shortly, "Out. He told me to tell you something. He said he was going to turn your old man over to the prison authorities in the morning. He changed his mind about makin' them extradite him."

"Why?"

The man grinned tauntingly. "Ask him."

"All right. I will." Cannon was making an effort to restrain the anger this deputy's taunting manner had raised. "Where is he?"

"See him later. He'll be back here at six. Now get the hell out of here. I'm busy."

Patience was at an end in Cannon. He crossed the room with a rush. He kicked the legs of the swivel chair viciously and it spun, yanking the deputy's feet off the desk, and spinning him helplessly. It rolled halfway across the room, Cannon following it. Every time the deputy spun to face him, Cannon slapped his face hard.

The chair stopped and the deputy came out of it, snatching for his gun. Cannon grabbed his arm and twisted. The deputy uttered a thin sound of pain and sucked in his breath. He tried to knee Cannon in the groin. Cannon stepped back and hit him flush on the mouth.

The deputy went backward, smashing against the wall with a crash that dropped two pictures from their nails in the wall. They hit the floor and both frames and glass broke.

A trickle of blood came from the corner of the deputy's mouth. He was not much older than Cannon, but his maturing had obviously been slower. Cannon thought he was going to bawl. The deputy's lower lip twitched and his eyes were wide with fear.

Cannon said, "Don't get tough unless you're tough enough to back it up. Now, where's the sheriff?"

"Over at Flora Curtice's place."

"Where's that?"

"It's a little white house on the street behind the hotel." The deputy licked his lips and made no move to get up. Lloyd Cannon, awakened by the commotion, came to the bars and looked at his son but he didn't say anything.

Stuart went out, his temper simmering. He rode toward the hotel and turned the corner beside it. He noticed John Redfern talking to a big, wide-shouldered puncher on the hotel veranda, but paid no particular attention until he noticed that they were both looking at him, obviously talking about him.

He looked away, his mind on the sheriff, and was almost past the hotel when the big puncher called, "Hey, you!"

Cannon turned his head. The man was approaching him at a swift walk. Cannon reined in.

The man said shortly, "Get down," and his belligerence was plain. Cannon shrugged and dismounted. He was a full head shorter than the big puncher and a whole lot lighter. He wondered what this was all aout.

He asked, "Sure you've got the right man? I don't know you."

The man said, "You will. I'm Tom O'Dell, foreman of Singletree." His quarrelsome manner was puzzling to Cannon. Cannon said, "You wanted something from me?"

"Yeah. Stay away from Eve Redfern."

Cannon's eyebrow raised. He was getting a little tired of hostility. His temper was crowding a ragged edge anyway over the way the deputy had behaved. He asked, "You own her?"

"Don't get smart with me, damn you! There ain't no room in this town for a woman-killer's kid. So get out, fast. And you don't see Eve again."

Cannon's eyes flared savagely with pure fury. But still he didn't move. He said softly, "I'm not leaving. And while I'm here I'll talk to whoever I blame please. So if you've got any chips, shove 'em into the pot."

He hadn't thought so big a man could move so fast. O'Dell stood with his shoulders hunched a little, his legs spread. He came uncoiled like a steel spring, and his beefly left hand came out and smacked like a sledge against Cannon's jaw.

Cannon's feet left the ground. He was flung backward like a limp rag doll. He went under his horse, but the animal was too well-trained to spook. He simply side-stepped until he was clear.

The instinct of a freight-yard brawler made Cannon roll, made him get his belly under him. The world revolved around him. He struggled to his feet, crouching, instinctively covering the vital places with his arms and ready to roll with any blow or kick that came at him.

He reacted as a hurt animal does, waiting for the return of strength and the will to fight.

But no blow came. He straightened, his head clearing. O'Dell stood in the same place he had stood before. He said, "Get out of Red Butte," quite obviously thinking this fight was over.

He was a tremendous, vital man who was used to ending fights with a single blow. Cannon gusted, "Oh, no! Huh-uh. Let's get our money's worth out of this!"

He knew those words were foolish even as he uttered them. He had been hurt by that first blow of O'Dell's. In addition to that he was plainly outclassed, by weight, by reach, by strength.

Yet he could no more have failed to utter them than he could have failed to get up.

His eyes sized up O'Dell in that instant while they stood facing each other. O'Dell was surprised and his surprise held him motionless for a precious instant while Cannon's head cleared.

Out of the corner of his eye, Cannon noticed the hasty approach of Redfern, of half a dozen others. Suddenly O'Dell became an object upon which Cannon could vent his frustration, his seething anger. He rushed, his arms working like pistons, smashing O'Dell's thick lips, his nose, raining upon his craggy brows.

242

The very fury of his attack made O'Dell back-step, off balance. Every ounce of power Cannon had possessed went into a blow which sank into O'Dell's belly and drove a grunt of surprise from the man.

O'Dell doubled instinctively, his hands dropping to guard his midsection. Cannon drove a savage right at his throat, which connected with a sound like that of a face being slapped. O'Dell's huge arm batted him away, and Cannon staggered for ten feet, fighting furiously to regain his balance.

He knew a feeling of helplessness, of something closely akin to fear. He'd put everything he had into that attack and he hadn't even dented the big man's assurance, much less hurt him.

But he'd made O'Dell mad, and at least that was a step in the right direction. He approached O'Dell warily, knowing he had to dodge the meaty impact of those beefy fists or be beaten in a matter of seconds.

O'Dell threw a whistling right that would have put Cannon out for half an hour. Cannon saw it coming, and for an instant thought he was too late to avoid it. O'Dell was fast, too damned fast for such a big man. Cannon's head came under the blow barely in time and it knocked his hat flying and grazed his head.

He countered instantly from his crouched position. He came up, using the rising drive of his legs, the power of shoulder and arm. His fist cracked against O'Dell's jaw with a shock that traveled clear to his knees.

O'Dell took three backward steps. His eyes blanked for the barest instant and his hand came up to rub his jaw. Cannon followed him, again raining blows into his face, blows which were largely wasted on the hand with which O'Dell now covered his face.

O'Dell backed another two steps with surprising quickness, and now both his fists swung wildly with a rhythmic flailing that Cannon could not for the life of him avoid.

A left against his shoulder drove him sideways, directly into a powerful, whistling right.

And for the second time, his feet left the ground. He hit the dusty street sliding, doubling even as he struck. He rolled, and came to hands and knees, his head hanging stupidly as for the second time he waited for the numbness to clear from his head. A brackish taste was in his mouth, a burning blindness behind his eyes.

He heard the shuffling approach of

O'Dell, sensed the savage kick aimed at his belly. He flung himself away from the kick even as it connected, and while it sent him rolling again, the force of it was largely lost. Even so, it made sharp pain shoot from his ribs into the pit of his stomach.

He gained hands and knees again, his head clearing. O'Dell stamped viciously at one of his hands, and Cannon yanked it away a split second before O'Dell's boot came down.

His head was clearing rapidly now, and as it did a kind of wildness ran through him. He drove his body upward against O'Dell's legs and felt them give, felt the man begin to fall. O'Dell sprawled across him, and Cannon's rising movement flipped him over onto his back.

Whirling, Cannon came down with both knees into the big man's belly. The heel of his hand came up against O'Dell's head, which he had raised several inches off the ground, banged back against it with a sound like a meat cleaver hitting the block.

And for the second time, O'Dell's eyes blanked.

Cannon came to his feet. His lungs were afire with their gasping need for air. His chest worked like a bellows, and the sound of his breathing was harsh and raspy, almost like sobbing.

Panic touched him as O'Dell began to rise. Beating O'Dell was like trying to split a boulder with a tack hammer. He'd thrown everything he had at O'Dell and hadn't hurt the man as much as O'Dell's first blow had hurt him.

Yet there was no retreat in him and no real fear. This was an old story to Cannon, who had beaten and been beaten countless times before.

O'Dell squatted, shaking his massive head stupidly. His lips were swelling, and blood ran freely from his nose. His eyes were red-rimmed, filled with a terrible fury. They were the eyes of a trapped, tormented wolf, of a hate-mad boar hog.

A low growling came from O'Dell's throat. He shook his massive head and struggled to his feet. He shambled toward Cannon, weaving a little, arms hanging straight down at his sides.

Cannon's next blow was a long shot, whose chance of success was slim. He drove himself forward, knowing he could break his hand on that massive, bony jaw, but knowing too that he had to have more force behind it than arm and shoulder muscle could give.

His legs were like pistons beneath him, driving him into motion, making his body surge forward. With all the weight of his driving body and its momentum, with all the powerful thrust of shoulder and arm behind it, his fist drove at O'Dell's jaw.

Pain shot through his hand and forearm as it connected. Shock traveled to his shoulder and numbed it. It was like hitting a stone wall with every ounce of power he possessed.

It stopped O'Dell, but it did not drive him back. Cannon ducked away, aware that his hand was probably broken, sure that he'd not hit O'Dell again with it in this fight. He knew he was finished, if O'Dell was not. The man could cut him to pieces now, in his own good time.

But Cannon had underestimated the terrible force of the blow he had just landed. O'Dell stood still, his eyes glazed, his jaw hanging slack, as though unhinged.

Suddenly those terrible, red-rimmed eyes rolled upward, and O'Dell's knees seemed to turn to jelly. He folded to the street without a sound sending little devils of swirling dust upward.

Cannon stood quite still, unbelieving, for a long, long moment. He heard the startled, awed talk that ran through the ranks of spectators. He knew he had been lucky, that except for chance it could well be himself instead of O'Dell lying there in the street. He also knew he'd have to face O'Dell again, and that next time the end could be quite different.

Tiredness weighted his body. His lungs, starved for air, worked like a bellows and his breathing made a whistling, sobbing sound. But, miraculously, he felt light and free. Bitterness had worked itself out of him during the fight. He found that he was grinning, though it hurt his jaw to do so. He looked around at the still-faced crowd and said breathlessly, "Anybody want to take it up?"

He got no answer, had expected none. Bravado had made him ask, but he knew he couldn't have whipped that fuzzy-cheeked deputy right now. He retrieved his hat, walked to his horse and picked up the reins.

So leaden were his muscles that he wondered if he could mount. He grabbed the saddle horn, put foot in stirrup and gave a mighty heave. He felt the saddle smack him.

The air was cool and sweet and good

flowing in and out of his lungs. He looked at Redfern, was surprised at the man's expression. There was astonishment in Redfern that the unbeatable O'Dell had been beaten. There was anger that it could have happened. And there was something else, that looked like panic, or fear.

Cannon nudged his horse and rode away at a quick trot.

## Chapter X
## Flora Curtice

He reached the corner before he remembered where he had been heading when the fight started. He looked for the white house, spotted it and headed toward it urging his mount gently.

It was a neat, small house, well cared for, recently painted. It had a white picket fence around its well-kept front yard, and an iron hitching post whose top was a cast horse's head. A horse was tied there and Cannon dismounted beside it and tied his own.

He kept trying to recall why the name of Flora Curtice had been so familiar to him and finally grasped it, recalling the snickers her name had always been able to start among a group of boys at school.

The house, then, was an incongruity. There must have been changes, in Flora Curtice as well as in the attitude of the town toward her. In the old days she'd lived in a shack out at the edge of town.

Cannon rubbed his jaw. It was sore, but he realized suddenly that O'Dell hadn't put a visible mark on him, save for a slight skinned place on the side of his jaw.

He mounted the steps and knocked on the door. An attractive woman in her early thirties answered the door. She looked at him questioningly.

Cannon remembered her as a blonde, but she was not blonde now. Her hair was warmly brown and was done in a restrained way with a bun low on the nape of her neck. She looked like any attractive wife might look and there was nothing about her reminiscent of her past.

She asked, "Yes?"

Cannon cleared his throat. "I'm looking for the sheriff. I was told I might find him here."

She smiled then, and her smile was quite warm. "Yes. Won't you come in?"

Cannon opened the screen door and stepped inside. Kearns sat on an upholstered horse-hair sofa, and he looked rather startled as he saw Cannon. He scowled and asked abruptly, "What do you want?"

Flora Curtice looked first at Cannon, then at the sheriff. She diplomatically left the room and went into the kitchen. Cannon said, "Your deputy said you'd changed your mind about making them extradite Pa. Why?"

Kearns straightened and sat on the edge of the sofa, elbows on knees, hands clasped between them. He said, "Redfern admitted to gettin' that gun to Lloyd. Said he did it out of friendship. It puts a different light on things."

Cannon was shocked, there was no denying it. He had made his mind up that a doubt as to his father's guilt existed, a hard thing for him, and now that doubt was being swept away. He asked, "What about the note?"

Kearns shrugged. "Somebody must have seen Redfern start the fire, or seen Billy Turk going into the jail. Redfern figures whoever it was didn't want to get involved, and wrote the note to avoid it."

"Then why wasn't the note addressed to

you? You could have taken the gun off Pa before he got a chance to use it."

Kearns shrugged. Cannon thought he detected resistance in the sheriff. He went on, "It's a nice pat explanation, isn't it?"

"What're you tryin' to say?"

Cannon felt anger stirring. "Suppose it was Redfern that wrote the note? His nice, pat explanation wouldn't do much good, would it?"

"I suppose not. But . . ."

Cannon interrupted, "Redfern just sicked his foreman on me. O'Dell told me to get out of town."

Kearns started. "Then you better git. He'll beat daylight out of you . . ."

"He tried."

Kearns sat up straight. He studied Cannon closely, showing plain unbelief. "You mean you've had a fight with O'Dell?"

Cannon nodded. He rubbed his jaw.

"And that's the only mark on you?"

"Except for skinned knuckles." He flexed his right hand, deciding now that it was not broken. If he could move it, it couldn't be broken.

Kearns stood up abruptly. "This is something I've got to see. Where's O'Dell now?"

"He was lying in the street at the side of

the hotel when I left him." Cannon would not have been human had he not felt a certain triumph in the telling.

The sheriff grabbed his hat, threw a look at Cannon and slammed out of the house. Flora Curtice came from the kitchen, and immediately, from the look on her face, Cannon could tell she had been listening. Her face was paler than it had been before and her eyes were no longer warm. She asked quietly, "You're Lloyd Cannon's son?"

He nodded. He looked at her for a moment, then he asked, "Are you ill? Hadn't you better sit down?"

She shook her head numbly. Her skin had lost all color and she looked as though she were going to faint. Cannon wanted nothing so much as to get out of this house.

He started to turn, but stopped as he heard her voice, very faint and low-pitched, "Why are you here? Why did you come back?"

Cannon said, "Pa escaped from prison. The priest at the prison asked me to come back and try to find him."

"Why?"

"The priest was afraid he'd be killed before he'd let himself be captured."

"What are you going to do now?"

It was a question which Cannon hadn't even asked himself yet. He didn't know. What he did know was that he wouldn't leave town in the face of O'Dell's threat and ultimatum. He said, "I'll stay awhile, I guess. Pa seems to have gotten the idea that he didn't do it. Maybe I'll stay and see whether he's right or not."

Flora Curtice was showing a lot of interest, he thought, and she was behaving strangely. Her eyes were fixed on his face, filled with something resembling terror. He wondered if she knew anything, and if she did, if she'd tell him what it was. He doubted it. If she had remained silent all these years she probably wouldn't change now.

He said, "I'll be going, ma'am. You'd better lie down awhile until you feel better."

"Thank you." Her eyes clung to him.

He wanted to shout, "What's the matter with me? Why are you looking at me like that?" But he clamped his jaw shut and went to the door. He looked back once as he went out. She had not moved, nor had her eyes left his face.

He stood for a moment on the porch,

aware that something was happening to him, but not understanding it at all. Then he turned in an abrupt rush and went back into the house without knocking.

Her wide eyes, in which such sudden terror leaped, confirmed his suspicions. He grabbed her by the shoulders and shook her fiercely. "Hang you, you know something! What is it? What are you so blamed scared of? You're not sick—you're scared because my name's Stuart Cannon."

"No! No! It's not true!"

"It is true!" Cannon could hear her teeth chattering. He said, "When I was a kid you had a shack down at the edge of town and nobody in town would have anything to do with you. Now you're up town and living in a nice house. It adds up to only one thing— blackmail. And it adds up to something else because there's only one man in the county with enough money to give you all the things you've got—John Redfern. He engineered a jailbreak to try to get my father killed. Has it occurred to you how dangerous it is for him to let you live? Particularly if I let word get out that you've promised to tell me everything you know?"

"You wouldn't!"

"I would. Unless you open up and tell

me what he's paying you for." Cannon couldn't quite conceal the triumph he felt at the success of his wild guess.

He was ashamed at what he had done to her—until he remembered that this woman had allowed his father to spend his life in prison when a few words from her would have freed him.

She said, "Redfern was in your house when your father came home that night. I was . . . I was standing in a doorway across the street with a man. I saw your father come home. He had been out of work for a long time and had got to drinking and he was drunk this night. He staggered against the fence and passed out hanging over it. Redfern came out and carried him into the house.

"He came back out and he happened to see me as he went by. The man I was with had seen none of it because he was facing me and because his mind was on me, but I'd seen it and Redfern knew I had. When the news got out next morning, Redfern came to see me and threatened me. He said your mother was still alive when he left, but that it would ruin him if it was known he was there. So I agreed to keep still."

"And that's all?" Excitement was rising in Cannon. When she nodded, he knew she had told all she knew.

"You'll be quiet about what I've told you?" Her terror was pitiful. Cannon nodded.

He went outside and headed for the jail. *Why? Why? What did Redfern have against my mother?*

He met Kearns returning along the street. In the sheriff's eyes was a kind of unbelieving respect. "I wouldn't have believed it, Cannon. I wouldn't have believed you could do it."

Cannon shrugged. "Never mind that. Just tell me, what connection did my mother have with Redfern? You were there. You ought to know."

The sheriff looked puzzled. "None that I know of." He shook his head. "Only time she had anything at all to do with him was the time his wife had Eve. Your mother went out there to help because the doctor was away."

"And that's all?"

"All I know about."

Cannon frowned. "Thanks," he grunted and moved away, thoughtful and preoccupied. It didn't add. There seemed to have been nothing between Redfern and Cannon's mother which would have been strong enough to provide a motive for murder.

How about Benoit? He had been at Singletree then. Maybe he'd remember something.

Or perhaps Lloyd Cannon might remember something, if properly prompted—something his mother had said, perhaps some worry she'd had.

He remembered suddenly that he had forgotten his horse and returned along the street to where it was tied before Flora Curtice's house. He untied the animal and mounted.

Bitterness and hatred, stored over the years, had built up a bank of debt that nothing but a lifetime could repay. Cannon was suddenly aware of the debt he owed Lloyd Cannon, of the debt this town owed too. He rode to the jail at a fast trot and dismounted before it. He went inside and looked across at his father, sitting dejectedly on the rumpled cot.

The downy-cheeked deputy scrambled to get his feet down off the desk. His eyes were wide, uncertain. Cannon said, "Get out of here. I want to talk to him."

The deputy started to bluster, his jaw firming out. Then, because Cannon's gaze rested on him so harshly, and because he remembered the last time he'd gotten smart with Cannon, he said uncertainly, "You'll get me in bad with Kearns."

"The devil with Kearns. Take your keys with you if it'll make you feel any better."

The deputy went out and sat down on the bench in front of the jail, turning his head so he could see what was going on through the window.

Stuart picked up a chair and carried it over to Lloyd Cannon's cell. He looked at his father, wondering how he could ever have thought of Lloyd Cannon as a black-bearded giant. His father was not even big, even though he was a little taller than Stuart himself.

Lloyd Cannon got up from the bunk and shambled over to the bars, his face holding nothing but defeat, and a pitiful sort of eagerness. He'd given up hope of proving himself innocent. The eagerness, Stuart knew, was only eagerness for a little kindness from his son.

For some reason Stuart's eyes burned and his throat felt sore. He coughed and said, "You didn't do it. I know you didn't. I can't prove it yet but I will. And then this town is going to make up to you all the years you spent down there." He drew a deep breath. "I'm going to try making it up to you too."

There wasn't much expression on Lloyd Cannon's face. But his eyes were awfully bright. He gripped the bars and his knuckles turned white. He was shaking all over. He croaked, "You've nothin' to make up, boy. The years ain't been easy for you, either."

There seemed nothing between them, nothing to make talk about. Prison had left its mark on the old man. It hadn't hardened him. It hadn't coarsened him. It had only bewildered and confused him. He lived now in a world all his own, where hurt and pain and regret were dimmed by distance. He tried to grin at his son and failed miserably. Then, because he couldn't seem to decide what to say or do, he shrugged and returned to his cot.

Stuart went outside. The deputy looked up at him and without saying anything got up and went back inside. Stuart rode down to Main and turned toward the hotel. He saw a woman, skirts lifted, climbing the steps to the hotel veranda, and at this distance she looked like Flora Curtice although he couldn't tell for sure.

Pressure troubled him. He knew what it was, but he didn't know what to do about it. Lloyd Cannon had only until tomorrow, when the prison guard would start back to the prison with him. Somehow Stuart couldn't stand the idea of his father returning to prison at all—at least until this thing was cleared up once and for all.

All right. Benoit was the last chance. His thoughts told him, *Get the devil out there and find out what Benoit knows. Even if you have to choke it out of him.*

Too many people hereabouts had been willing to let an innocent man go to prison. Too many people had been afraid, or greedy, and Lloyd Cannon had paid the bill. It was time someone paid him back.

## Chapter XI
## The Reason

Riding out toward Benoit's shack, Cannon kept mulling the puzzle over in his mind. There had to be a connection between Martha Cannon and Redfern. There had to be a connection which would provide a motive strong enough for murder. And yet what possible motive could there be for Redfern to kill a woman who had simply helped out while his wife was having her child? And how could such a motive carry over until ten or twelve years later?

If there was an answer, Benoit would have it, for he had been at Singletree when Eve was born. In fact, if Stuart remembered the stories he'd heard as a boy, Benoit's wife had had a child at about the same time, a child which died.

Despondent over the loss of her firstborn, and perhaps unbalanced to some degree as well, Benoit's wife had killed herself. It was what drove Benoit mad, folks said, if he was mad.

Unable to put the puzzle together with so many pieces missing, Cannon dismissed it from his mind. He began to think of Eve, and there was a certain longing in his thinking.

Eventually he brought Benoit's shack in sight, and rode up to it openly, thankful now that he had intervened in Benoit's trouble with Turk a couple of nights ago. Perhaps there would be enough gratitude in Benoit to make him willing to talk.

Stuart hailed the shack, and Benoit came

to the door, the wolf leashed at his side. Cannon could see the old man's fright fade as recognition came to him. Cannon said, "I'd like to talk to you. I think I can clear Pa if you'll tell me all you know about Redfern and my mother."

A curtain seemed to drop over Benoit's eyes. He stooped and released the wolf, which darted at once for the brush.. Cannon's horse must have gotten a smell of him, for the animal began to buck savagely.

Cannon rode him out, and when he was again able to control the animal, dismounted and tied him securely to a clump of brush.

Benoit stood aside to let him enter. The rank odor of confined animals struck Cannon, and he said, "Let's talk outside. Those blamed cats make me nervous."

He squatted beside the wall of the shack and rolled a cigarette. He said, "There's someone in town who saw Redfern come out of our house the night my mother was killed. My father came home about the same time and passed out draped over the fence. Redfern carried him inside and then came back out himself. I've got reason to believe that Redfern might have killed my mother and that Pa's spent all these years in prison for something he didn't do. But I can't think of any reason Redfern might have for killing her. Can you?"

Benoit's eyes were guarded, careful, frightened. But they were not mad, nor were they blank. He shook his head.

Stuart went on, "Near as I can find out, the only time Redfern had anything to do with my mother was when his wife had Eve. You were at Singletree then. Did anything happen that might give him a reason to hate my mother?"

Again Benoit shook his head, but now there was pain in his eyes.

Cannon said quickly, "Didn't your wife have her child at about the same time?"

Benoit's muscles gathered. He started to run, but Cannon's hand came out and grasped his ankle. Benoit fell headlong, kicking to be free. Cannon held on. He said, "Damn you, I helped you out the other night when Turk had a rope on you. You're going to help me out now if I have to sit on you 'till you do."

Benoit's struggles stopped, but Cannon did not release him. Cannon said, "Didn't she?"

Benoit nodded. Cannon asked, "How near the same time?"

Benoit's voice was a croak. "Same day."

"Wasn't that kind of queer? Two women having babies the same day?"

Benoit shrugged. "They weren't supposed to. Your mother was out at Singletree to help my wife have her child. Mrs. Redfern's was not expected for another month. But she fell downstairs, and the child was born too soon."

"But it was your wife's child that died?"

"Yes." Cannon saw suddenly that Benoit understood what he was getting at. Cannon felt sure he was on the track of something now. He asked urgently, "Who was with your wife and Mrs. Redfern when they had their babies?"

"Just your mother. The doctor was away from Red Butte."

Cannon knew he was guessing. But he said, "Suppose it was not your daughter at all that died, but Mrs. Redfern's? Isn't that logical in view of the fact that she fell downstairs? And suppose that Redfern bribed or persuaded my mother to exchange them?"

There was a dead silence while something wholly wild and unmanageable was born in Benoit's expression.

Cannon went on hastily, "Wait. Don't jump to conclusions. Let's work this out."

265

Benoit said, "You can let me go. I will not run away."

Cannon released him. He spoke in a soft, almost musing tone. "Mother took his money, maybe because she needed it badly. She went back to town. Then your wife killed herself, and you turned kind of wild. Mother probably blamed herself for your wife's death, for your condition too. The years passed, and the load of guilt got too heavy to carry. Maybe she told Redfern that she was going to tell. Now what would you do in a fix like that if you were Redfern?"

"Not what he did!"

Cannon got to his feet. "I'm going back to town. You coming?"

Benoit nodded.

"Want to ride double?"

"No. I'll run along beside you."

Cannon untied his horse and mounted. By the time he kicked the horse into movement, Benoit was already three hundred yards away in the direction of Red Butte. Cannon ranged up alongside of him and drew his horse into a trot. Benoit kept up, running tirelessly the way a wolf or a dog runs. His bare feet made a gentle, padding sound.

Cannon wanted to spur his horse into a

wild gallop, but he restrained himself. He had until tomorrow. Lloyd Cannon was not due to leave for the territorial prison until then.

"There might have been a good many reasons for Redfern to exchange the babies," Cannon said as though thinking aloud. "One might be that he didn't want his wife blaming herself on account of that fall. Maybe that was the only reason. But after your wife killed herself and you left Singletree, he probably got so he liked running it all by himself. He probably got attached to Eve, too, and didn't want to lose her. He knew if my mother talked that Eve would hate him and that you'd come back to take over your part in managing the ranch. Besides that, he'd be forever disgraced in the Giant's Graveyard. He'd lose the position he values so."

*It all fitted*, thought Cannon. It fitted almost too perfectly. But it was the only explanation that did fit.

He didn't know quite what he intended to do. He only knew that he had to face Redfern to accuse him. He'd know from the expression on Redfern's face whether he was right or not. After that, he'd have to play it by ear. It would be up to Redfern how it went from there.

# Chapter XII
## A Long Story

It was late afternoon when Benoit and Cannon reached Red Butte. Cannon reined in before the livery stable. His horse was tired and he knew the animal had earned a rest and a feed of grain. He looked at Benoit, whose only sign of his long run was his soft, even panting. "Wait here a minute. I'll put my horse up and then we'll go see Redfern together."

Benoit nodded and leaned against the wall of the stable. His wildness seemed to have left him altogether. There was no blankness in his eyes, no apparent fear of the town or the townspeople. Yet there was another expression in his eyes that troubled Stuart, for it was wild, unmanageable, unpredictable.

Stuart led his horse into the cool, shady livery barn and slipped off the saddle. He rubbed the animal's sweaty back with a gunny sack. Then he led the horse back to the same stall he'd had last night and dumped a generous measure of oats in the

268

feed box. Leaving the horse quietly feeding, he went outside.

It was the supper hour, which explained the absence of an attendant at the stable. It also explained the absence of townspeople on the street.

Cannon looked around for Benoit, but Benoit was gone.

A vague uneasiness stirred in Cannon. Why the devil couldn't Benoit have waited? And where could he have gone?

Cannon remembered the unpredictable look that had been in Benoit's eyes, and began to walk at a fast pace toward the hotel. There could only be one place Benoit might have gone—Redfern's room at the hotel. And Benoit was unarmed and virtually defenseless.

If Cannon's guesses about Redfern had been correct, Benoit was now in grave danger. He began to run.

He burst into the hotel lobby. He took time for a hasty glance inside the hotel dining room. Then he took the stairs two at a time with scarcely a glance for Eve Redfern, who rose from the settee in the lobby and stared at him with startled fright.

He judged that Benoit could not be more than five minutes ahead of him, but a lot could happen to a man in five minutes. Five minutes was long enough for a man to die. Redfern, with his back to the wall, would be no more squeamish tonight than he had been the night of Martha Cannon's death.

Cannon ran along the hall and without knocking, burst into Redfern's room.

Benoit lay on the floor, crumpled in a wholly lifeless position, and from a nasty gash on his head, blood had oozed onto the worn red carpet. Redfern, gun in hand, stood over him, his eyes holding a crazy, trapped fury.

Immediately as Cannon burst in, Redfern's gun swung to cover him. Some of the trapped look faded from his eyes, and his lips split into a wolfish grin. "Well! Now I've got the two of you. And that's all I need, you realize that, don't you? Because Flora will go right on keeping her mouth shut just as she's been doing for years."

Cannon was inwardly cursing himself for his stupidity in entering Redfern's room with his gun holstered. He ought to have known better.

Redfern, his gun unwaveringly on Cannon's middle, said suddenly, sharply, "Turn around! Fast, damn you!"

Cannon hesitated. He saw the tendons in

Redfern's hand tighten. His shoulders lifted in a helpless gesture of defeat, and he turned slowly.

His body was tense, and suddenly his back began to ache in expectancy of Redfern's bullet striking it. Redfern said harshly, "Walk over to the wall. Raise your hands and clasp them behind your head. Quick! Move damn you!"

Cannon did. He knew he was closer to death right now than he had ever been in his life.

He debated making his try now, for he had no assurance that Redfern would not simply shoot him down in cold blood. With Redfern's position and wealth, the man could probably cook up some story which would be accepted. Redfern could claim that Cannon had killed Benoit, and that he had shot him in the back as he was leaving.

Cannon's muscles tightened. He would have thrown himself aside, but before he could the door burst open and Eve stood framed in the doorway. "Father! What's the matter? What's going on here?"

There was the smallest instant while Redfern groped for an explanation while his attention was wholly diverted from Cannon.

271

In that instant, Cannon acted. He whirled and drove across the room.

No time to draw his gun. No time for anything but hurling himself at Redfern's legs.

The gun muzzle dropped. The gun roared out in the closed, confined space. And then Cannon's body struck Redfern's legs and both went down in a tangle of wildly thrashing arms and legs.

He had Redfern's gun wrist in an iron grasp, and twisted viciously until Redfern gasped with pain and released the gun. Cannon snatched it up and came to his feet. He said breathlessly, "Eve, sit down. This is a long story and it's not very pretty. It started a long time ago, the day you were born."

He halted long enough to catch his breath. Redfern sat on the floor, looking up at him as though stunned.

Cannon went on, "Mrs. Redfern and Mrs. Benoit had baby girls on the same day. My mother was out at the Singletree helping. But due to a fall downstairs, Mrs. Redfern's baby died. Redfern persuaded my mother to help him exchange the children. You were taken from your own mother and given to Mrs. Redfern, who never knew you were not her own.

"You know what happened. Mrs. Benoit killed herself and Benoit left Singletree and took to living like a hermit. But as time went on, my mother's guilt became too much for her to bear. She told Redfern she was going to confess.

"He couldn't afford that. So he killed her. Flora Curtice saw him come out of our house that night. She saw him carry my father inside, unconscious. Redfern has been paying for her silence all these years."

He looked at Eve. Her eyes were wide, unbelieving. She said, "You're lying. It isn't so."

He stared at her steadily. She must have seen from his expression that he believed what he said, for a certain, fearful doubt entered her eyes. He said, "I've got Redfern's gun. I'm going to get the sheriff and Flora Curtice. I'm going to have Pa out of jail and Redfern in it before the night's over."

He took the key from the inside of the door and stepped into the hall. He closed the door behind him, locked it and pocketed the key. He knew he couldn't trust Eve to go for the sheriff. In her confused state, she would naturally believe Redfern innocent. Instead of going for Kearns, she'd pick up the first member of the Singletree crew she saw.

He ran down the hall and took the stairs two at a time. He crossed the lobby, ignoring the curious crowd, and ran into the street.

The sun was setting now. Cannon ran toward the sheriff's office, Redfern's gun still in his hand, forgotten. Lord! He'd been so wrong all these years. He'd been so terribly wrong.

Behind him, he heard a window come up, heard Redfern's shout, "Turk! O'Dell! Dutch!"

For an instant concern touched him, but it immediately went away. Redfern was hooked. He'd never talk himself out of this one. And he wasn't, Cannon thought, the kind who'd try to fight his way out of it.

He met Kearms coming out of the sheriff's office. Quickly, before Kearns could see it, he stuffed Redfern's gun into his belt. He stopped the sheriff and launched into his story breathlessly.

Kearns listened with irritated incredulity. But as the story progressed, doubt entered his tired old eyes.

At last he said, "You say Redfern killed Benoit?"

Cannon nodded. Kearns showed instant concern. He said, "And Redfern was yelling for Turk and O'Dell when you left?"

Again Cannon nodded, at last seeing what Kearns was getting at. Kearns broke away from him and began to run. "Then we'd better get over to Flora's place and darn quick. Because she's the only witness left against Redfern."

Cannon caught up with him before he reached Main. Together then, they ran toward the hotel. Cannon noticed that the upstairs window from which Redfern had yelled was now empty.

As they rounded the corner and headed for Flora Curtice's house, Cannon began to pull ahead. Suddenly, from behind Flora's backyard fence, a gun roared, and a puff of smoke revealed its position.

Kearns yelled, "Down! For Judas' sake, get down. They'll get you before you go fifty feet!"

Another gun puffed, and a fraction of a second later, its report reached Cannon's ears.

But now his gun was in his hand. He swerved sharply, and headed directly for the fence. The two men who had been behind it now got to their feet, sure of him, sure they could cut him down before he could reach the fence.

Redfern. Where was Redfern? Cannon felt a cold touch of fear. Because he knew that Redfern had left these two outside while he went in. Even now Flora might be dead.

Kearns must have thought the same thought, for he paid no attention to the pair behind the fence, Turk and O'Dell. Cannon triggered a shot at Turk, deeming him the most dangerous of the two, but it missed.

A bullet tugged at his sleeve, and a second took his left leg out from under him. He sprawled in the dust, sliding, holding his gun high so that the muzzle would not fill with dirt.

He saw the smoke billow out from O'Dell's gun muzzle, and stiffened against the bullet, which showered his face with blinding dust and dirt.

Then the two were vaulting over the fence, their faces grinning in sudden triumph.

Cannon rolled and thumbed back the hammer on his gun. Snap shooting, he fired at O'Dell and saw the man halt, saw a dazed, shocked expression touch his face, then saw him crumple slowly into the street.

A bullet from Turk's gun plucked the gun from Cannon's fist and left his hand bloody and numb. Still lying in the dust, he rolled and with his left hand, snatched Redfern's gun from his belt.

Turk, shooting from eye-level now, carefully aiming, thumbed back the hammer for the final shot that would smash through Cannon's head.

And Cannon, in desperation, snap-shot Turk as he had O'Dell.

For a moment, he thought he had missed. Then, as he waited for the impact of Turk's bullet, the man's gun hand began slowly to drop. Turk's gun clattered to the street and he began to fold.

Before he hit the street, Cannon was crawling toward the house. Redfern. There still was Redfern.

Shots echoed like firecrackers from inside the house. The back door opened and Flora ran out, screaming. She crossed the back yard and disappeared into the rear door of the hotel, directly across the alley.

Somewhere behind him, Cannon could hear another woman screaming.

She seemed to be crying a name, a name that sounded like "Stuart!"

Consciousness began to slip from Cannon. He saw the tall, old form of the sheriff come from Flora's back door, smoking gun in hand. And then there was a flurry beside him and Eve was down on her knees in the street, lifting his head to her lap.

She kept saying, over and over, "Where are you hurt? Where does it hurt?"

Cannon grinned, feeling good for the first time in years. Hatred and bitterness had dropped from him like a cloak. He looked beyond Eve and saw Benoit staggering toward him, holding a bloody rag against his cut scalp.

Eve turned and followed his glance, and smiled uncertainly. "No. He wasn't dead. He was only knocked out. But fath . . . Redfern didn't know that."

Cannon's grin softened into a smile. Because the hard, bitter, hating years were past. The ones ahead would be good, good for himself and Eve. And best of all, good for Lloyd Cannon.

He looked up at Eve's face, into her tear-bright eyes. What he saw there must have satisfied him, for he finally relaxed and let the pain and shock of his wounds claim him. All he needed now was rest and a quick recovery, so that at last he could begin to live.

279

# Hell-Bent

## Chapter I
## The Range King

He stopped at the top of the ridge and looked back down, a broke, dispirited and sour man in his early thirties. Below him Spade lay, stretching from where he sat to the horizon, taking in the wide, watered valley dotted with brown haystacks that at this distance looked like fat loaves of bread.

He stopped and looked back, did Ernie Parfet, and through his bitterness seeped a puzzled wonder. Because it was unbelievable.

As long as he could remember he had lived on Spade, and now he was going away. Strangers would ride the scattered ranges. Strangers would inhabit the house in which Ernie had been born. Maybe they'd cut Spade up and sell it off to the settlers that jammed the town of Wild Horse.

He looked across the valley, up from the

silver thread of creek winding erratically through the hay meadows. He looked at the timbered slopes beyond at the grassy park that dotted their secret fastnesses. He looked at the dark red spots that were the cattle grazing.

He was a broken man, who now had two courses lying before him. Give up and drift out of the country. Or stay and fight it out. Stay and try to start anew.

Spade was gone and could never be recovered. The old way of life was gone. Behind Ernie's saddle were all his worldly possessions, tied up in his blanket roll. His horse and his saddle, his roll of blankets, and the things he retained of spirit and ability were all that were left.

Ability? He laughed mirthlessly, bitterly. What ability was there when you could begin with a ranch like Spade and end up broke? They'd broken that. The way you take an outlaw horse and break him until his head droops and his eyes turn dull.

Angrily he yanked his mount's head around and touched spurs to the animal's sides. And so went over the ridge and out of sight of Spade.

He went toward Wild Horse then, neither hurrying nor lagging, and his mind was like

281

a trapped animal exploring a cage for a way out.

He was broke. Literally broke. He had a handful of change and that was all. He was lucky to have his horse, his saddle and the clothes on his back. Bankruptcy courts were unsympathetic and thorough.

But he had friends. And a man could find the way back if he wanted to find it hard enough.

Short of the town he halted and fished automatically in his pocket for tobacco. He made a cigarette, absently noting that the sack was two-thirds empty.

A job would be first, and it was with this thought in mind that Ernie Parfet headed for the Horsehead Saloon. Next to Spade, Ike Pearce's J Diamond outfit was the largest, and Ike could usually be found in the Horsehead.

The Horsehead sat between the Western Hotel and Garrity's Saddle Shop. It was a frame building, two stories high, and on its front was painted a horsehead and underneath that the word "Saloon."

Ernie Parfet shouldered his way inside.

There were three men at the scarred oak bar. Three more were playing poker at one of the tables. From the back room came the click of billiard balls.

And there was an odd restraint in all these men as Ernie came in.

Ike Pearce was one of those at the bar, an oldish man, heavily grayed and balding. His eyes were bright blue and his thin lips showed a secret, sour mirth. He needed a shave. Ernie nodded to him and moved up to the bar at his side. "Hello, Ike."

Ike nodded shortly and without much warmth.

Ernie said, "I'd like to talk to you."

"What about?" Ike turned and threw the bartender a wink. Ernie felt a stir of anger, so great was the change in Ike Pearce's manner.

Ernie said stubbornly. "You know about Spade. I need a job, Ike."

Ike laughed drily. "Doin' what?"

"Riding." Ernie's anger was rising, but he held it under tight control. Ike said, raising his voice so that it carried well, "By Judas, Ernie, after the way you managed to lose Spade, that's all anybody'd let you do."

Ernie muttered, "It's all I'm asking. A job." Ike was making him feel like a beggar. He reminded himself bitterly, *It's what I am. I'm broke and I have to eat.* But he could not hold back his resentment. There should be nothing shameful about a man asking for a job. Yet Ike made it seem shameful.

There had been a time when Ike had not been like this. When Spade was Ernie Parfet and Ernie Parfet was Spade, Ike had acted differently toward him. Ernie guessed now sourly that Ike was one who rode high with you when you were riding high, then kicked you when you were down.

Ike turned to the bartender. "Give the Range King a drink, Sam."

Sam looked at Ernie. Ernie fished in his pocket, found a quarter among the small amount of change he had and rang it on the bar. "I'll buy my own, Ike."

Ike laughed mockingly. "You'll change. Six months from now you'll be hanging around in here sponging drinks from anyone who's fool enough to buy you one. I know your kind, Parfet. You had Spade handed to you when your dad died, ready-made and running. You've had things easy all your life, and you won't be able to stand it any other way. You'll go to hell fast, Ernie, maybe quicker than most."

Ernie's face reddened with anger and his fists clenched at his sides.

This only seemed to amuse Pearce, who said, "You'd like to hit me, wouldn't you, Ernie? All right. Go ahead. I'm little enough so that you ought to be able to kick daylight out of me. And that'll make you feel big again, won't it, Ernie?"

Ernie Parfet could see the way it was going. He could see that the loser, whatever happened, would be himself. He wanted to get out, but he didn't want to run. He picked up his drink and carried it to his mouth.

Just at that instant, as though by accident, Ike Pearce moved. His elbow came out and jostled Ernie's arm violently. The whisky slopped from the glass, over Ernie's chin, and across the front of his shirt. Its reek came up strong and acrid to his nostrils.

Even so, it might have been all right if Ike hadn't laughed. Ernie might have maintained his control except for that. But Ike did laugh, harshly, mockingly, nastily. And Ernie lost his head.

He didn't hit Ike. But he put his hand on Ike's chest and pushed, saying, "If you're so blamed clumsy stand a little farther away."

Ike tripped over his own feet and sprawled on the floor. As though at a signal, the other two with him, J Diamond's foreman Rufe Fahr and a big puncher Ernie didn't know, came in swinging.

Rufe's right fist smashed against the side of Ernie's jaw. With the force of Rufe's running rush behind it, it slammed Ernie back against the bar with a crash. The big puncher came from behind Rufe, eyes shining, and followed Rufe's blow with one of his own, one that landed against his teeth.

Ernie shoved himself upright, keeping his back to the bar, shaking his head to clear it. He could see the three who had been playing poker at a nearby table coming now, and in them all was the plainly seen desire to get a lick at Ernie while the getting was good.

Ike Pearce came up off the floor, spluttering as though he had fallen into the icy water of Crooked Creek. He shrieked, "Get him, Rufe! Get him good!"

Two of the poker players came in from Ernie's side. Rufe and the J Diamond puncher from the other. The remaining poker player came in from the front, and Ernie caught this one with a long, looping left, flush to the point of the man's jaw. The man went down with a choking gasp and lay still for the moment, stunned.

But Ernie was momentarily off balance. Rufe gave him a stiff jolt to the kidneys and the poker players' punches landed almost simultaneously, one on the side of his neck, the other high on his head. Ernie's right lashed out and smashed Rufe's nose, drawing a gush of blood and bringing tears to Rufe's eyes. He followed that, for Rufe was the aggressor in this, but the puncher's outstretched foot came between Ernie's feet and sent him sprawling to the floor.

They were on him, like a pack of dogs on a luckless cat, kicking, kneeing, wildly swinging.

Their blows landed in Ernie's hard, flat belly, his chest, his throat. They smashed into his face. He rolled his head and a kick landed on the back of it, a kick that had been aimed at his face.

Ike kept jumping up and down, yelling frantically, "Get him! Get the son!" But the sound of Ike's voice was dimming from Ernie's consciousness.

Oddly, the punches that were landing didn't hurt anymore. There was only their stunning, jolting force.

Ernie knew he was going under. He put everything he had into throwing them off, using all his strength, all the force in his body. He came to his knees, gasping, using fists and elbows, and felt them falling away.

He came to his feet and backed from the tangle of their struggling bodies on the floor. He laid his elbows on the top of the bar stool and stood, glaring, drawing deep, choking breaths of air into his starving lungs.

He made a sound like a bellows, and blood streamed from a dozen gashes on his face. One eye was already beginning to swell, and his mouth was a bloody pulp. Through it, he said with difficulty, "Now, let's start over, damn you. Let's begin again."

He shoved himself away from the bar, a roaring sound in his ears. He held his clenched fists loosely at his sides.

The tangle on the floor resolved itself into men, scrambling to their feet, glaring and coming in, but cautiously this time. Ernie felt a fleeting satisfaction seeing the damage he had done.

Ike Pearce snatched a shot glass from the bar and flung it. It caught Ernie high on the forehead and glanced off, breaking a bottle on the backbar.

The glass was heavy and had been flung

with considerable force. Instinctively, Ernie took a backward step and reached back to the bar for support.

Behind him, the bartender swung the barrel of his shotgun, and it slammed into Ernie's head like an iron club.

Slowly, silently, Ernie sagged. His eyes glazed. He hung with desperate strength by his elbows from the bar for a moment, and then even these went limp and he collapsed to the floor.

Ike stepped up then and kicked Ernie until he was pulled away.

## Chapter II
## The Hate

It was a long, hard climb from unconsciousness for Ernie. First he heard sounds, voices, the run of a horse's hooves in the street, the distant cry of a child.

He heard a groan next, never realizing that he had made this sound himself.

He stirred and felt the thousand aches and pains in his battered body. He licked his lips and found them swollen and scabbed.

Lastly, he opened his eyes and was surprised to find it dark save for the lamplight that laid a barred pattern on the wall across from where he lay.

He stayed still, half drugged by the deep unconsciousness from which he was just now emerging. And heard a voice he recognized, the voice of Spence Cole, the sheriff. It said, "Joe, I'm going home for supper. I'll bring something back for Parfet, but I don't reckon he'll be able to eat much tonight."

Ernie heard a scuffle of booted feet and the slam of a door. Cautiously, carefully, he swung his legs over the side of the smelly bunk and sat up.

Now a thousand sledges pounded at his skull from the inside. His vision blurred and swam. But he held tightly to his newfound consciousness, and after a while things steadied and became still before his eyes.

Lastly, as was inevitable, his anger came. Why was he in jail? He had done nothing but defend himself against an unwarranted and long-odds attack.

But anger made his head pound worse. He put up a hand and felt of it gingerly. There was a lump on one side of his head. This must have been the one which knocked him out, he thought.

There were others, some of them scabbed

with dried blood. Ernie made a sour frown and called, "Joe."

He heard the swivel chair in the outer office creak. Joe Boggs, the jailer, appeared at the bars of Ernie's cell.

Joe was a little man, wizened and cheerful. He said in his cracked and reedy voice, "You finally come out of it, hey?"

Ernie asked harshly, "What the devil am I doing here? Hang it, unlock that door and let me out."

Joe shook his head, his grin disappearing. "Huh-uh. You got to get used to something, Ernie. You ain't Spade no more. You're just an ordinary guy. You disturb the peace an' you land in jail. You was drunk an' quarrelsome. You wrecked a couple of things at the Horsehead, an' if you don't pay for 'em, you don't git out."

Ernie throttled his anger and asked softly, "What'd I wreck, Joe?"

Joe crossed to the desk and picked up a scrap of paper which he brought to the bars of the cell. He squinted at it and finally said, "Broke three bottles of whisky. Broke a chair. Broke the stock of the bartender's shotgun. Ernie, I'd like to 've seen that fight. You was doin' all right." He peered at Ernie, unsmiling. "Damages come to thirty-three dollars. You want to pay it now, Ernie?"

Ernie stared at him bleakly. He said, "Ike broke one bottle behind the bar with a shot glass he heaved at my head. The bartender must've wrecked his own blamed shotgun knocking me out. Chances are one of those poker players broke the chair in his hurry to get out of it and take a swing at me."

"Ike an' the bartender say you done it. Two agin one, Ernie. An' like I said, you ain't Spade no more."

No. Ernie was discovering that the hard way. He wasn't Spade any more. But he wasn't an ordinary guy, either. He was a man that everybody wanted to kick, to push down into the mud.

Joe Boggs repeated, "You want to pay up, Ernie?"

Ernie fished in the pocket of his jeans. He came up with a handful of change and counted it. Four dollars and eighty-seven cents. He shook his head. "You'll be a long time getting it out of me, Joe."

He lay back down on the bunk and stared somberly at the ceiling. His head ached and his vision was fuzzy. He tried to think.

How had he gotten into this shape in the

first place? How could Spade have gone so far downhill that there was nothing left?

It had started about three years ago, he remembered. A killing winter of blizzard after blizzard. Cattle had drifted, had piled up on barbed wire fences and died like flies, one upon the other until a man could walk over the top of the fence on their frozen bodies.

Spade had lost two-thirds of its cattle that winter.

The following year had been one of drouth, for after that winter snow not a drop of moisture had fallen for four long months. The range had dried up. The bed of Crooked Creek was dusty dry, smelling of rotting fish and stagnant water.

As though that were not enough, blackleg had come to Spade's range and had taken what few cattle the drouth did not.

So Ernie went to the bank, mortgaged Spade for enough to start anew. He took a crew and went to Texas. He came back driving two thousand gaunt, tough cattle. He sent to Missouri for fifty Hereford bulls.

That fall the cattle market fell apart. From thirty dollars, the price of a steer went to seven. And the bank closed in.

After that it was long days in the bankruptcy court. Ending with the loss of Spade. Ending this way, in Wild Horse's stinking jail, beaten and bruised and simmering with futile anger. Wanting revenge against Ike Pearce for putting him here and stacking the cards so that Ernie would have to stay here.

Ernie made a low, bitter laugh. What was it he had been thinking as he rode toward town today? That he had friends? That he could start fresh here in Costillo Country? That he could live so long as he was willing to work?

He came out of his musing, hearing voices in the sheriff's office. Joe Boggs' voice, and a woman's lighter tones.

Ernie sat up abruptly and the sledges began to beat against his skull. He recognized the woman's voice as Fay Kingman's. She was saying, "How much damages does he owe, Joe?"

"Thirty-three dollars."

"Here. Now will you let him go?"

"Sure, Miss Fay, Sure." Joe's steps came toward the cell door and a key clicked in the lock. The door swung open on squealing, protesting hinges. Joe said, "You're bailed out, Ernie."

Ernie looked up. He felt sheepish, ashamed. You are a long ways down road when you have to depend on a woman to pay you out of jail. He got to his feet and went out, at once faintly angered at the look of compassion that crossed her face. Her eyes, meeting his, were filled with painful embarrassment. But she only said, softly, "Come on, Ernie. Supper's on the table. I'd have been here sooner, only I didn't know."

Joe had to get in a last lick as Ernie followed her out the door. "Ernie. Better stay out of trouble."

Ernie didn't answer, and the only indication that he heard was the deepening color on the back of his neck.

The night was cool, and a yellow moon was rising in the east, magnified by dust in the air. Ernie walked beside the girl in silence.

She was a tall girl, coming a little above his chin. Her hair was glossily black, her forehead smooth and untroubled. Her gray eyes asked no question that her lips did not, and for that Ernie was grateful. But his hurt pride made him ask, "Aren't you going to ask me what happened?"

"It isn't my business, Ernie. You're hurt

and you needed help. That's enough for me."

He said stubbornly, "I want to tell you. I didn't go into the Horsehead looking for trouble, Fay. I went in to ask Ike for a job. It must have made him feel pretty big. Anyway, I found out how much he hated me and hated Spade."

She murmured, "It's a kind of envy, I suppose."

"I guess so."

"What will you do now?"

Ernie considered for a moment. They came to Kingman's house and paused by common accord beside the white picket gate. At last Ernie said, "I won't let them run me out, if that's what you mean. Somewhere in this country there's a job for a man, even one like me. Somewhere there's bound to be someone that doesn't hate Spade. And if there isn't, then, I'll make a job for myself. I'll run wild horses on the mesa."

Fay Kingman said softly, "Come on in, Ernie. I'll bandage those cuts on your face and then we can eat."

# Chapter III
## One Lightning Stroke

Ike Pearce stood at the bar for a while after Ernie was carried out, listening to the gleeful run of satisfied talk around him. He felt a certain satisfaction over the way Ernie had been mauled, but his hatred of Ernie and Spade was too deep for that to completely satisfy him.

Ike Pearce had lived on the rim of gigantic Spade for most of his life. He had seen Spade prosper and grow while his own J Diamond outfit stagnated, while he himself merely eked out a living.

In the early years, he'd had more than one run-in with old man Parfet over range, and water, and an occasional handful of Spade cattle that disappeared and were tracked to J Diamond by Spade's riders.

And so, through the years, Ike's resentment and hatred of Spade had grown.

Spade's bankruptcy and Ernie Parfet's loss of it eased his hatred somewhat, but did not completely satisfy it. Only Ernie Parfet's personal ruin could do that.

He left the bar and idled into the back

room where he racked up the billiard balls and began playing rotation by himself. After a while that palled, and he went back into the bar and got into a poker game.

He played through late afternoon hours and into the early evening. And he drank steadily, though his drinking seemed to have no visible effect upon him.

All this while his brain was busy. Ernie Parfet was in jail, and would probably not get out until he made arrangements to have the trumped-up damage claim paid.

At suppertime, Ike got himself a snack from the Horsehead's free lunch counter and went back to his game.

And so the evening hours went and closing time came. It was then that Ike's idea came to him as he watched Sam Shultz stow the day's receipts into an already bulging wallet which he carried in his inside coat pocket. Sam left the small change and silver dollars in the money drawer behind the bar.

Sam yelled at the sparse crowd, "All right, you guys. You can carouse all night, but I can't. I have to open up tomorrow. Come on, I'm closin'."

The half a dozen men in the saloon filed reluctantly out the door, Ike with them. Sam came out and locked the door behind him. The two of them stood on the walk for a moment, and finally Sam said, "Night, Ike," and turned away toward home.

Ike watched him go. He knew the route Sam always took toward home. It was cut through the narrow passageway at the side of the Horsehead. Down the alley to its end. Then west along Fourth and north on Mustang to his small bachelor shack at the edge of town.

Ike hesitated but for an instant, hearing the weeds in the passageway rustling as Sam made his way through them.

He was thinking that it would be difficult in the morning for the sheriff to accurately decide the time a man had died the night before. He was thinking that he'd go down to the jail after this was done and bail Ernie Parfet out himself, saying that his anger over the fight had cooled now and that he would, out of friendship, pay the damages done in the Horsehead.

Moving swiftly at a shambling running walk, he went along Main northward. He passed Fourth and saw the black shadow that was Sam Shultz moving along it, his back toward Main. Ike hurried a little more. He passed Fifth and came to Sixth. He was openly running now along the deserted street, staying in the street's dust to muffle the sound of his pounding boots.

He came to Mustang ahead of Sam Shultz, and ducked down, panting behind a sagging picket fence. He dragged air deep into his lungs, both to quiet the sound of his breathing and to still the frantic pounding of his heart.

Sam seemed to move toward him with agonizing slowness, a mere black shadow in the street. He was half a block away now, shuffling along like a man tired from his day's work.

Ike wondered again, briefly, how much was in that wallet. He began to chuckle soundlessly. This was vengeance against Spade and Ernie Parfet and profit for himself all in one lightning stroke.

Ike didn't worry about Sam. Sam was only a means to an end, and tonight not a person at all.

But Ike could feel the tension mounting within himself. Sam must not be allowed to cry out. There must be nothing, nothing heard and nothing seen that would place the time of Sam's death with any accuracy.

Sam came abreast of him, muttering softly to himself. He seemed preoccupied with something, some private thought, and so had no eyes for the black shadow behind the fence.

Ike let him go by, and then stood up silently, easing his gun from his hoslter. Like a cat, he ran along behind Sam, raising the gun as he did.

His boots made a soft scuffling noise in the dirt, for there were no boardwalks along Mustang Street. And at the last moment, Sam turned, saying with startled fright, "Who's that? What—?"

Ike brought the gun barrel down in a vicious, slanting arc. It thudded solidly against Sam's skull. It thudded solidly and sickeningly and Sam collapsed to the ground.

Ike stood over him for a few moments, fighting for control of his shaking hands. He looked upstreet and down, seeing nothing, hearing no sound. He stooped, felt Sam's chest for heartbeat. It was slow and erratic.

Kneeling on one knee, Ike reversed the gun in his hand and brought its heavy butt deliberately down on Sam's head. Again and again, with a kind of brutal frenzy now giving no heed to the fact that Sam was stone dead.

At last Ike gained control of himself, and breathing hard, holstered the gun.

Again he looked up and down the street. Then his hand went into Sam's inside coat pocket and withdrew the wallet. He stuffed it into his own pocket, got ahold of Sam's skinny body under Sam's arms and dragged him over behind the fence.

Moving away, he satisfied himself that Sam's body was not readily visible, then hurrying, went back along the way he had come.

Short of the hotel, he paused, stooped and wiped his bloody hands on a clump of long grass.

The clerk looked up from the desk in the hotel lobby as he came in, grinning, "Horsehead closed, Ike?"

"Yep." Ike climbed the stairs wearily and went to his room.

Once there, he lighted the lamp, poured water into the washpan and washed his hands. There were splashes of blood on his clothes, so he took them off and put on fresh ones, thankful that he kept a change here in town.

Then with a final checkover in front of the mirror, he went out and back down the

302

stairs. The clerk looked up curiously. "Going out again, Ike?"

Ike made his grin sheepish. "I got ready for bed, and then I got to thinking of Ernie Parfet. I guess I'll go down and pay him out of jail."

The clerk looked at him with startled admiration. "Takes a big man to do something like that, Ike. But you needn't bother. Fay Kingman done that early this evening."

Ike made no effort to hide his relief. He sighed and said, "Well, I'll be going up to bed then." And chuckling soundlessly, he climbed the stairs.

## Chapter IV
## Hard Man to Pin Down

Fay Kingman lived with her aged, childish father. She taught school for a living, and worried greatly when she was gone during the day for fear her father would injure himself.

He was an inveterate pipe smoker and was careless with matches, careless too about where he knocked out the coal in his pipe.

She gave no thought to propriety or to what the town would say when after supper she told Ernie, "Sleep in the back bedroom tonight, Ernie."

He shook his head. He was thinking of the barn loft out in back of the house and said, "No. But I'll sleep out in the loft if you don't mind."

Fay flushed as she understood the reason for his reluctance. But she nodded in assent. "If that's what you want."

Ernie was weak, and tired now. The maximum effort he had put forth in the saloon fight, plus the beating he had taken, had sapped nearly all his strength. He stood up, pushed his chair back under the table and stood looking down at Fay. He said soberly, "You're a real friend, Fay."

For an instant her eyes were soft, defenseless, and told him plainly, "I would like to be more than just a friend, Ernie." He looked away, embarrassed.

A couple of years ago he had courted Fay almost constantly, taking time out from the management of Spade to come to town often. The winter during which so much Spade livestock had died had halted his courting. For one thing, it was almost impossible to get from Spade to town that winter because of deep snowdrifts and bitter cold.

For another, Ernie and every Spade hand

had been busy. Endlessly and urgently busy trying to save what they could of Spade's dwindling livestock.

The following summer had been one of drouth and of blackleg, and had left Ernie little chance to visit Wild Horse or Fay Kingman. After that there had been the trip to Texas for replacement cattle, and then the falling livestock market and the closing in of Spade's creditors.

Ernie had been ashamed to court Fay after he had seen the way things were going. He hadn't felt he could ask her to marry him when he had only himself to offer her.

He grinned at her faintly, and murmured, "Good supper, Fay, I'd forgotten what a good cook you are."

"Thank you, Ernie." There was coolness and some embarrassment in her tone.

Ernie grinned again and headed for the door. Fay sprang up and left the room, calling, "Wait, Ernie."

He hesitated at the door and after a moment she returned, carrying an armload of blankets which she handed to him.

Ernie went out the door and crossed the yard to the barn. It was yet early, but Ernie was tired. So he climbed to the loft, spread his blankets on the hay, and lay down. And was almost instantly asleep.

He awakened with the glare of sunlight in his eyes. And with the sound of voices in his ears.

For a few dazed moments he stared around him, trying to decide where he was. He moved, and pain raced through his bruised muscles. Then he remembered. The fight in the Horsehead, jail, Fay Kingman's getting him out and taking him home to supper. He remembered that he was up in the barn behind Kingman's house.

He recognized the sheriff's voice below in the yard, probably at the back door. "We're lookin' for Ernie, Miss Fay. You got any idea where he went?"

Fay's voice was bitterly accusing. "Why don't you let him alone? He told me about that fight in the saloon. He didn't start it, Ike Pearce did. And there were six men fighting him not counting Sam Shultz. What do you want with Ernie now? I paid the damages you claim he did in the Horsehead."

The sheriff mumbled something and Fay repeated sharply, "Why do you want Ernie? What are you going to accuse him of this time?"

The sheriff's voice was clear and cold as he answered. "We want Ernie for murder, Miss Fay. Last night he killed Sam Shultz and took Sam's wallet."

For an instant there was only shocked silence below in the yard. Ernie could feel his body growing cold. Someone was out to get him, that was plain enough, and this time it looked like they were going to succeed.

At last Fay's voice came, low, and filled with outrage. "How do you know Ernie did it? Did someone see him? And if they did, why didn't you come after him last night?"

"He did it all right." Sheriff Spence Cole's voice was positive, angry. "He was sore at Sam for knocking him out with that shotgun. He was sore about that trumped-up damage . . ." His voice stopped guiltily.

Fay cried, "Then it was trumped-up, just like Ernie said!"

Cole's voice was rueful. "Well, yes. But Ernie was sore about it. So he laid for Sam and beat him to death. You got any idea where he might've gone, Miss Fay?"

Fay's answer was low, but Ernie heard it plainly enough. She said, "No. I haven't the faintest idea. I loaned him a horse right after supper and he rode away."

Ernie's heart sank. Fay was trying to help him, but she just hadn't thought quickly enough. In trying to save him from capture she had thrown away all chance of giving him an alibi.

Ernie was instantly ashamed of that thought. Why should Fay lie to alibi him? Indeed, why should she try to protect him at all? She owed him nothing.

Tense, really scared for the first time in his life, Ernie listened to the sounds of the sheriff and his men leaving. And he heard the lawman call back, "We'll get him, Miss Fay. We'll get him before we're through."

Ernie stayed utterly still until all sound of their going had faded. His heart was pounding frantically. He had to get away—far away—and at once. He had to put miles between himself and Wild Horse, between himself and the vengeful townspeople.

He rolled out of his blankets and stood up, and instantly his body set up its protest at this sudden movement. Ernie hobbled to the ladder and climbed down onto the barn floor. The sheriff, believing him guilty of killing Sam, had not even thought of doubting Fay's word, of searching the premises for him.

He went to the door and looked out. Fay

was watching the retreating form of the sheriff and the men with him. When they turned the corner she came at once to the barn and stepped inside. Her eyes were wide with terror. Her lips formed the words, "You heard him?"

Ernie nodded. He said, as if to forestall the question he knew would appear in her eyes. "I never stirred last night."

She said reproachfully, "I didn't ask you, Ernie."

"No. I know you didn't." He stared at her steadily for a moment while his mind raced frantically. Panic tugged at his thoughts, and all he could think of was getting away. He muttered, "I've got to have a horse. A fast one. I've got to get out of this country."

"If you didn't do it, you've nothing to worry about."

Ernie laughed harshly, "Don't be foolish, Fay. You saw what they did to me last night."

She stepped close to him and her hands closed tightly on his arms. "Ernie, stop it! What have you got if you run? Even if you're lucky enough to get away? Running will be a confession, and after that, you'll be wanted for the rest of your life."

He said sourly, "What have I got if I stay? Do you think there's even a chance I won't hang for this?" He laughed bitterly. "Ike Pearce set out to cook my hash last night in the Horsehead . . ." Ernie stopped, knowing suddenly that only one man in Wild Horse could have killed Sam Shultz. Unless this was just a disastrous coincidence—that Sam's killing had just happened to occur last night. He repeated, "What chance have I got? The whole town seems to have hated Spade, and this will make them all feel good."

Fay said gently, "Someone killed Sam."

"Sure. Ike Pearce probably. But who'll believe that? Who'll believe that I didn't?"

Her voice was firm, if a little unsure. "Nobody, unless you give them a chance to believe you."

He was incredulous. "You mean you want me to stay?"

"Today. Maybe tonight. I'm not asking you to give yourself up, Ernie. Just stay until . . ." She did not finish.

Ernie was beginning to see some sense to her suggestion. For one thing, during the next twenty-four hours the country would be swarming with men looking for him. If they didn't find any trace of him they'd give up, and then it would be safer for him to leave. But it was not for this reason that Fay wished him to stay. She had hope of clearing him, and Ernie knew there was no hope.

Fay turned away, her face troubled. "I've got to get over to the schoolhouse. If I don't show up, they'll suspect something. Will you stay hidden until I get back?"

Ernie nodded doubtfully. "I'll try. But Fay, I'm warning you. I won't let them take me."

She searched his face with her eyes for a moment. Behind him in the stalls the two Kingman horses fidgeted and stirred. From the street came the faint sounds of children's yells as they ran toward the school.

She murmured, "I've got to go." But she seemed to be waiting for something. She took a step toward Ernie Parfet. "Ernie . . ."

He closed the distance between them. His arms went out and closed around her. For an instant he held her close, and then he spoke to her fragrant hair, "I neglected you, Fay, but it wasn't because I wanted to. There was that hard winter when we lost so many cattle. Then there was the drouth and the blackleg. Then the trip to Texas for replacement stock. After that I was ashamed to ask you to marry me. Because I didn't have anything but myself to offer."

Without raising her head, she said, "I never wanted more than that."

He said harshly, "I can't even offer that now."

She laughed shakily. "You're a hard man to pin down, Ernie."

Between them was silence for a moment. Then she raised her face. "Ernie, kiss me, so I can know, one way or the other."

That was puzzling to Ernie, but he lowered his lips. The kiss was light at first, cool. A kiss of gratitude and friendship. But it did not remain that way very long, for between them, in both their hearts, a fire kindled and burned hot and fierce. Passions that had lain dormant these past few years burst to the surface. Ernie's arms tightened savagely.

But Fay pulled gently away. Her eyes were shining, her lips smiling triumphantly. She said, "Wait for me, Ernie. I'll see you tonight." And she went out of the barn into the bright sunlight.

He watched her go and knew an empty sense of loss. For he could not be sure he would see her again.

# Chapter V
## No Other Way

The morning hours dragged by. Ernie climbed the loft and lay down in the fragrant hay. He was hungry, and thirsty, but afraid to go out.

From time to time he heard a shout in the town, or the drum of horses' hooves in the street. These were the sounds of activity that told him the search for him was not abating.

Once, old man Kingman came out and drew a bucket of water from the pump.

This was the first time Ernie had seen the old man for a couple of years, and he was amazed at the change. Old man Kingman seemed to have aged ten years in the last two. He was frail and thin and he staggered a little under the weight of the bucket.

Ernie supposed the reason he had not seen the old man last night was that he had gone to bed early. Ernie wondered if Kingman were aware of his presence here, and if he were, wondered if he'd stay quiet about it in case some of the sheriff's men came snooping again.

Ernie went back as soon as Kingman disappeared into the house, and laid down again. His mind wrestled with his problem, coming up with no new answers, with no solution but flight.

In spite of what Fay Kingman thought, Ernie knew he had no chance at all here in Wild Horse. People were too prejudiced. After the fight last night, and the twisted accounts of it that had been circulated, they'd be only too ready to believe him capable of killing Sam Shultz for his money.

The trial would be a farce. Circumstantial evidence would be enough to convict and the jury would be loaded with men who already believed him guilty.

Frowning, he closed his eyes. The fragrance of dry hay was heavy in his nostrils, and gradually he became drowsy.

He slept, and in sleep, sweat popped out on his face and his face twisted with the torture of his dreams. He was being chased, his horse exhausted and stumbling, while those of his pursuers were fresh and fast. Bullets whined around his head as he laid low over the neck of his faltering horse.

The animal stumbled and went to his knees, catapulting Ernie over his head, rolling. Ernie came up with his gun in his hand. And found himself kneeling in the barn loft's hay, at last aware that it had been a dream.

He grinned shakily and brushed the sweat from his brow. And then became aware of the noises in the yard below.

There was the steady creak of the pump, the frantic shouts of men. Many men. There was the scream of a woman, "He's in there! Dad's in there!"

Ernie frowned with puzzlement, recognizing Fay Kingman's voice. And then he heard it. The crackle, the low roar of flames.

Below in the stable, Ernie could hear the frantic stamping of the two horses, their shrill nickering. He smelled the acrid, over-powering smell of smoke as the wind changed and blew a cloud of it toward the barn.

Someone yelled, "Get the horses out of the barn! That'll likely go next!"

Ernie walked carefully to the wall and peered through the crack into the yard. There were perhaps a dozen men down there, as many women. But the men were the old ones, the ones who had been too old to take the trail after Ernie Parfet. The young men of the town, the ones who might have brought the blaze under control, were out riding the country searching for Ernie.

The house itself was enveloped with flame. Already the roof was smoking and would in a few moments burst into flame itself. The back door was effectively barred by an impenetrable wall of fire and smoke.

The men and women in the yard had formed a bucket brigade between house and pump, but the effect of their flung buckets of water was negligible. The house was lost, and everything in it. Now all they were trying to do was to save the town. And chances of that appeared slim, for as soon as the roof of the Kingman house caught, then sparks would soar away in the wind and shower the town.

Ernie saw Fay look once at the barn, her face white, her eyes wide and filled with pain and entreaty. Then, before he could move, she ran toward the house.

They caught her a yard from the back door. Caught her and held her, screaming and fighting, crying hysterically, "You can't let him burn! You can't just stand here and let him burn!"

It took two men to drag her away. Two men to hold her after they did.

Ernie hesitated not at all after that. He ran across to the ladder and went swiftly down to the barn floor. He opened the door a crack and looked out into the yard.

The bucket line was continuing, but the glances of all were turned toward the struggling girl and the men that held her. Ernie burst from the barn and crossed the yard, running, toward the house.

The silence of shame hung like a pall of smoke in the yard as Fay continued to scream, "Please! Please! Someone go after him, or let me go! Please!"

A gruff man's voice said loudly, "It'd be suicide, Fay. Crazy. Nobody could go in there and come out alive."

And then someone saw Ernie. A shout raised, "It's Parfet. Get him!"

A shot racketed and the bullet tore into the porch ahead of Ernie. Ignoring that, he snatched a bucket from a startled woman and dumped it over his head. It soaked him thoroughly. He snatched a shawl from another woman's shoulders and dipped it hastily into the bucket she held. He wound it around his face, covering mouth and nose and tied it swiftly behind his head.

The shooting had suddenly stopped and a strange silence hung over the yard. Ernie lunged toward the back door of the house, but then suddenly he remembered his gun and cartridge belt. The heat of the flames might explode some of the cartridges. So he unbuckled the belt and let it drop.

As he stepped into the flames, heat seared his hands, his face. Steam from his soaked clothes scalded his body. The last sound he heard over the roar of the flames was Fay's shriek, "Ernie! Oh Lord, not you too!"

The porch floor, burned through, collapsed under Ernie's weight and he plunged through, recovered and clawed his way onward. The burning boards seared the palms of his hands. The pain was excruciating.

He might not have had the courage for this, he told himself, if he had not already been lost, if he had not been doomed to death already. There is something about fire that terrifies a man as it does an animal. Because he is helpless in its grasp.

He went on, into the churning, boiling smoke of the kitchen. He yelled, "Kingman! Where the hell are you?"

He stopped, coughing, listening. His skin felt as though it were on fire, stretched like shrinking hide over his face. He grimaced. His eyes slitted against the acrid smoke, he

318

staggered across the kitchen and went on into the parlor.

Here the fire had apparently started, for this room was a mass of orange flame. It threw off light, but smoke dissipated the light and Ernie could not even see the far wall of the room. The heat was becoming unbearable. Ernie's lungs were a mass of pain as they fought for life-giving air and found none.

Dizziness clutched at Ernie's consciousness. He felt himself falling.

He went to his knees, staggered up to his feet and went on. If Kingman were in this room, Ernie knew he was dead. No man could live here for more than a few short seconds.

Ernie tried to remember the arrangement of the rooms, tried to recall where the doors were that opened off the parlor into the bedrooms. He brought up with a crash against the far wall and groped along it.

He found a door, a closed door, and put his hand on the knob. It burned, and he snatched his hand away with a savage curse. But he had to get through. He had to search each room in its turn.

Deliberately he returned his hand to the hot metal. And opened the door.

Cooler air blasted him in a rushing gust. Flame and smoke followed him into the room, but not before he saw the limp, collapsed shape of a man on the floor.

There was a window on the far wall, but it was small and high. Ernie assessed the difficulty of hoisting Kingman out of it and decided he had not the strength. So it was return by the way he had come. There was no other way.

He knelt beside Kingman for a moment, while his lungs drew deep breaths of this purer air that lay close to the floor. He snatched off the damp shawl from his face and tied it over Kingman's.

Then he grabbed the slight body of the old man beneath his armpits and dragged him toward the door.

What followed was a nightmare that Ernie would forever remember. He could not walk, nor stand erect. His strength, sapped by the treatment he had received yesterday in the Horsehead, was rapidly waning.

So he crawled, and dragged Kingman over the hot floor behind him.

He went through the parlor and the trip seemed to take hours, though it could have been only seconds or minutes at most. He went through the kitchen, and at its door encountered helping hands, for the fire fighters had drenched the way across the porch with water and had laid new planks across its burned-through timbers and flooring.

They dragged Ernie out and dragged Kingman out after him.

Ernie lay gasping, spent, in the yard.

He was conscious, but he could not move. He heard Fay Kingman's voice and felt her hands against his face, cool and cheerful. He heard her shriek for the doctor.

And he heard another yell, one that brought him recognition and a stir of hatred. He heard Ike Pearce's scream. "There he is, Sheriff! Arrest him! There's the man we been hunting for. There's the one that killed Sam!"

Ernie struggled, fought for consciousness and strength. He sat up. He could see that the crowd in the yard had increased. In some way, the posses scouring the country for him had been apprised of the fire and returned to fight it. Already their efforts were becoming apparent.

They'd drenched the walls and roof of the barn so that it would not catch from the house, and stationed watchers with wet sacks on the roofs of nearby houses. The fire would not take the town, but that was little help to Ernie. He was wanted and he sat there helplessly waiting for them to take him, having not even a gun with which to fight.

## Chapter VI
## The Killer

Ike Pearce yanked out his gun and flung a shot at Ernie. It missed, but it showered him with dirt as it struck the ground close by. Ike yelled, "Take him, damn it, or I'll kill him!"

Somebody grabbed Ike and his gun went off again. But this time it was pointed directly at the sky. Half a dozen men jumped him and tore it from his grasp. Ike screeched "Ernie killed Sam! You going to let him get away?"

The sheriff growled angrily, "He ain't going nowhere. Now shut up, Ike."

A lot of things were adding up in Ernie's mind. He'd suspected Ike of killing Sam, but he hadn't been sure. Now he was. Ike had never been one to demand punishment so rapidly for lawbreakers before. He'd broken the law plenty himself. And he hadn't been a particular friend of Sam's.

Ernie shoved the doctor aside and stood up. He staggered. The sun on his burned skin was torture. He croaked, "I didn't kill Sam. I was asleep in the barn loft last night. But I think I know who did."

Ike struggled helplessly in the grasp of the men that held him. Ernie walked toward him, saw a panicked fear in Ike's small eyes. He said softly, "You did it, didn't you, Ike? So I'd be blamed for it?"

"No! Hell no! You can't get out of it by accusing me!"

Ernie said, "Sheriff, search him. Sam was killed for the money in his wallet you said. If Ike did it, the wallet will either be on him or in his room at the hotel."

The sheriff looked skeptically from Ernie to Ike and back again. He said, "He wouldn't be damn fool enough to be lugging it around."

"Maybe he would. Maybe he's just sure enough that everybody'll think I did it that he wouldn't worry about being accused himself."

Still the sheriff hesitated. Out of the corner of his eye, Ernie could see the doctor working over the prone shape of old man Kingman, and he saw Kingman stir.

He knew what a slim chance this was. He knew that in all probability, Ike had hidden the money-laden wallet. And he knew that except for the fact that he had dragged Kingman out of the burning house, no one would even have listened to him.

Fay Kingman cried, "If nobody else will do it, I will," and she moved toward Ike.

The sheriff stopped her. "Get back, Fay. I'll take care of it."

She whirled on him savagely. "Then take care of it! So Ernie can get over to the hotel and get to bed. So the doctor can take care of him. He's taken about all one man can stand!"

Ernie watched the face of Ike Pearce. He saw the thin lips working beneath the face's untidy coating of whiskers. He saw fear in Ike's eyes.

The sheriff must have seen this too, for he asked soberly, "Which pocket, Ike?"

"Inside coat pocket," Ike said surprisingly, and licked his lips as the sheriff withdrew the wallet. His eyes turned crafty and sly. "But I didn't kill Sam for it. I took it off his body. I seen Ernie kill Sam, but Ernie didn't take the money. So after he left

I took it. That's why I didn't come running and report that Sam was dead."

Ike was breathless, pale. He was talking for his life now and he knew it. Ernie asked, "Sheriff, what was used to kill Sam?"

"Gun butt, probably."

"Look at Ike's then. Maybe he didn't get it all cleaned off."

One of the men holding Ike withdrew the gun from Ike's holster and handed it to the sheriff. The sheriff looked down at the steel butt. There was a rusty stain on it, visible even to Ernie. The sheriff plucked a couple of hairs from under the walnut grips where they had lodged. He said harshly, "This does it, Ike, you're under arrest for the murder of Sam Shultz. Take him down to the jail, boys."

For the briefest moment, surprise held all the spectators to this, held them motionless. The grip of Ike's captors must have relaxed for an instant, for the wiry little man broke free with a violent wrench. He snatched his gun from the sheriff's surprised hand and whirled to face the crowd, backing toward the barn as he did.

A boy got in his way and Ike grabbed the boy and snarled, "Get me the sheriff's horse."

The boy looked at the sheriff, frightened, questioning. The sheriff said, "Do it, boy. Go ahead."

Ike snarled, "Now, Ernie. Now." He raised the gun.

Ernie could hear the rustle of movement as people behind him moved aside. He heard Fay scream, sensed her rushing toward him. There was only one thing to do and he did it. At a shambling run, he went toward Ike, expecting momentarily the smash of Ike's slug into his body.

But he had reckoned without the sheriff. And the rush toward Ike had given the sheriff the split second he needed. Ernie diverted Ike's attention from the rest of the crowd just long enough. Ike's gun blasted and a terrible force struck Ernie's shoulder and half spun him around.

But the sheriff's gun was speaking too. Once. Twice. And when Ernie turned back, looked at Ike, the man was slipping inertly to the ground.

Suddenly all the strength was gone from Ernie. He saw the horizon tip, saw the sky whirl crazily above him. And he felt the ground at his back. He could hear the shocked murmur of the crowd and the soft crying of a girl. He could feel her tear-wet face against his.

Ernie forced a grin to his burned face. He said, "Neither of us have got a roof over our heads now. But in a day or two, I'll do something about that."

She was really crying then, but she was laughing too. And to Ernie, Spade no longer mattered at all because he had found something that more than took its place.

# Acknowledgments

"Too Good with a Gun." Copyright © 1950 by The Hawley Publications, Inc. First published in *Zane Grey's Western Magazine*.

"Massacre at Cottonwood Springs." Copyright © 1950 by Ziff-Davis Publishing Company. First Published in *Mammoth Western*.

"Dobbs Ferry." Copyright © 1950 by Fiction House, Inc. First published in *Frontier Stories*.

"High Carded." Copyright © 1950 by Lewis B. Patten. First published in *Western Short Stories* as "Fast Draw Feud."

"Nester Kid." Copyright © 1950 by The Hawley Publications, Inc. First published in *Zane Grey's Western Magazine*.

"Payday." Copyright © 1951 by The Hawley Publications, Inc. First published in *Zane Grey's Western Magazine*.

F.

The publishers hope that this
Large Print Book has brought
you pleasurable reading.
Each title is designed to make
the text as easy to see as possible.
G.K. Hall Large Print Books
are available from your library and
your local bookstore. Or, you can
receive information by mail on
upcoming and current Large Print Books
and order directly from the publishers.
Just send your name and address to:

G.K. Hall & Co.
70 Lincoln Street
Boston, Mass. 02111

or call, toll-free:

1-800-343-2806

*A note on the text*
Large print edition designed by
Kipling West.
Composed in 16 pt Plantin
on a Xyvision 300/Linotron 202N
by Stephen Traiger
of G.K. Hall & Co.